T0204845

THE POWER OF LOVE

Conventional life has never been easy for Hannah Lavender. Her sister Ronnie is an activist in a commune, and her mother Babs has suddenly left her housekeeping job with geo-thermal engineer Steve Talbot, eloping to America with a Texan cowboy. Hannah is drafted in to take her mother's place as housekeeper, but it doesn't take Ronnie long to super-glue herself to a protester outside Steve's front gate. When Babs joins the protest, Hannah is forced to flee the job and the man she loves.

MARGARET MOUNSDON

THE POWER OF LOVE

Complete and Unabridged

LINFORD
Leicester

First published in Great Britain in 2013

First Linford Edition
published 2015

A catalogue record for this book is available
from the British Library.

ISBN 978–1–4448–2263–2

Published by
F. A. Thorpe (Publishing)
Anstey, Leicestershire

Set by Words & Graphics Ltd.
Anstey, Leicestershire
Printed and bound in Great Britain by
T. J. International Ltd., Padstow, Cornwall

This book is printed on acid-free paper

1

'Will you keep your voice down?'

Hannah glanced nervously over Steve Talbot's broad shoulder. The chief librarian was making tea but it was well known that she could hear a pin drop at twenty paces. Any hint of a disturbance and she would be out of the staff room quicker than lightning.

'Where are they?' Steve lowered his voice a fraction. His blue eyes were as cold as shards of ice.

'I don't know,' Hannah gulped.

This wasn't the first time her mother had got her into trouble and she doubted it would be the last.

'Not a good enough answer.' Steve had plonked himself in front of the main desk and looked as though he had every intention of staying.

'It's the only one you're going to get.'

It took a lot to rile Hannah but so far

it had been the Monday morning from hell.

There had been an important meeting over the weekend and all the staff had been asked to stay behind after the library closed for a special briefing. Those on holiday or on a day off had also been called in.

Rumours about cutbacks were flying thick and fast. Hannah knew she was in real danger of having her hours cut or worse. She loved her work and didn't want to lose her job, but she had been late for work yet again that morning, something that had not gone unnoticed by Miss Lawrence.

Hannah had missed one bus and the next one was cancelled. By the time she raced up the library steps to open up, there was a long queue outside and several of the regulars were grumbling about having to stand around waiting in the rain.

'When I entrusted you to open up, Hannah,' Miss Lawrence told her after she had called her into the back office,

'I placed my confidence in you as a responsible member of the team. It would seem my trust might have been misplaced.'

'I'm sorry, Miss Lawrence,' Hannah had apologised. She tried to explain but Miss Lawrence was not in the mood for excuses, and with cheeks flaming Hannah had scuttled back to the desk.

She wouldn't have been late if Lucy hadn't played up, saying she felt sick and not eating her breakfast. Then on the way to school she pretended to have a tummy ache and dragged her feet as Hannah urged her along. At the school gates Lucy had spotted her best friend in the playground and, forgetting all about her phantom tummy ache, raced towards her, not bothering to kiss Hannah or to wave good-bye. Fuming, Hannah had trudged through the puddles back to the bus stop just in time to see the bus taillights glowing red in the distance as it accelerated away. It had been a thirty-minute wait for the next one.

As things were settling down into some form of normality, Steve Talbot had stormed through the library doors, a thunderous look on his face. 'Where is your mother?' he demanded, looming over the desk.

Hannah had in the past found his presence overwhelming, but today she was in no mood to be intimidated by this bully of a man who seemed to think if he raised his voice loud enough he could browbeat her into submission. The time had come to make a stand. The trouble was, like Steve, Hannah actually had no idea of her mother's exact whereabouts.

Babs Lavender was a sixties wild child who thrived on the challenge of the unexpected. Hannah couldn't count the number of times her mother had dragged her off somewhere on a whim to a holiday, or a party. On one occasion they had wound up on a yacht. The next thing Hannah knew, they were sailing across the channel all set for a wild weekend in Le Touquet.

'Darling, it will be fun. Lighten up,' Babs would laugh. 'At times you can be the teeniest bit stuffy.'

As soon as Hannah was old enough to dig her toes in and refuse to play ball, Babs would take off alone — and that was exactly what she had done this time, only she hadn't been on her own. She had tried to persuade Hannah to go with her, but she had told her mother she had no intention of playing gooseberry.

'Have you tried asking Ronnie where she is?' Hannah ventured.

The look Steve cast Hannah brought a flush to her face. The last time Steve and Ronnie had encountered each other, her sister had been heading up a peace protest, chanting and brandishing a placard telling the world exactly what she and her fellow protesters thought of geothermal engineers.

Steve had done his best to quell the action and explain that he was one of the good guys looking for sustainable ecological ways of drawing heat from the ground, but Ronnie was doing what she loved best in the world, protesting, and reasoned explanation was not going to stop her. A heated altercation had followed. In the ensuing chaos Ronnie's placard had been ground underfoot, and the undignified episode that followed was another one Hannah would rather forget.

'Perhaps that was a silly suggestion,' she admitted.

'I should have known better than to employ your mother.' Steve ran a hand through his scrubby dark brown hair. It was in need of a trim, Hannah noticed. 'But I had no choice.'

'There's no need to make my mother sound like the last resort,' Hannah bridled at his criticism.

'Sorry,' Steve apologised under his breath.

Hannah's twinge of sympathy for his plight deepened. He hadn't shaved recently and his eyelids were drooping from lack of sleep. She didn't doubt he worked hard. He was never in one place for long and according to her mother, it wasn't unusual for him to be called up in the middle of the night and told to make off to some far corner of the world at no more than a moment's notice.

'I thought you weren't due home for another week,' she said.

'There was a last-minute change of plan and as I've run out of clean socks, I thought it was time I dropped by to pick up some fresh laundry and check on the house.' There was a thud as his holdall landed on the library carpet tile. 'So if it's not too much trouble I'd like to know what's happened to my house keys.'

Babs Lavender had been employed as Steve Talbot's housekeeper for six months. For all her wayward ways, she was more than qualified for the post. Having been widowed at a young age and with two daughters in tow, she had been forced to earn her living taking jobs that provided accommodation. Her cooking and cleaning skills were in high demand and until her daughters had grown up she could pick and choose positions. True to her nature, though, she never stayed in one job for any length of time.

'I need to take off to the beach every summer,' she would explain to her daughters, 'and build snowmen in the winter if I feel like it.'

Ronnie had loved the lifestyle. Hannah hadn't. Every time she thought they had settled down, her mother would start to get itchy feet and they would be off on their travels again.

'I haven't seen my mother for a few days,' Hannah began to explain.

'She hasn't gone off on another of her jaunts, has she?' Steve demanded.

Although Hannah didn't know where her mother was, she knew what she had been doing. 'We weren't expecting you back so soon,' said, evading a direct answer, 'otherwise I'm sure she would have been here.'

'Are you? Are you really?' Steve looked as though he didn't believe a word of her story. Hannah couldn't blame him. It was difficult to sound convincing when you weren't a very good fibber.

'I only have myself to blame I suppose,' Steve said. 'I mean it's not as if your family's history isn't known to me.'

Hannah squirmed and hoped he wasn't going to start on about Ronnie. She would feel honour-bound to defend her sister, but to be frank this morning she wasn't sure she was up to the task.

A loud cough interrupted their exchange. Hannah's spirits sank even further when she saw who the new arrival was.

'I'm sorry to interrupt.' Patricia Morris looked anything but sorry. 'Only, I'm due at the dentist's in ten minutes. I can't wait all day.'

'You can check your own books out now, Mrs Morris.' Hannah summoned up a smile for the local busybody who loved nothing better than to poke her nose into other people's business. She didn't doubt the woman had overheard every word of her exchange with Steve. This latest drama was grist to her mill. 'The machines are over there. All you have to do is scan your book. I've shown you how to do it several times.'

'I can never work those wretched things.' Patricia waved a bejewelled hand dismissively. 'Besides, what are you assistants here for, I'd like to know? You stand around all day, gossiping. It's my opinion you haven't got enough to do.' Her eyes strayed in Steve's direction.

'I wasn't gossiping,' Hannah began.

'Hello, Mrs Morris,' Steve joined in. 'As you can see, I'm back. You can spread the word around town that Hannah and I have already had a heated exchange about her mother's whereabouts and that as a result I am temporarily locked out of my house. Now if you'll give me your book.' He took it from her unresisting fingers, scanned it under the reader and handed it back to her in the space of seconds. 'There you are. No need to be late for your dental appointment, is there?' He glanced at the title. 'You'll even have time to read your lurid blockbuster in the waiting room after you've imparted all the latest gossip to the receptionist, won't you?'

'Well, really.' Patricia Morris stiffened in outrage. 'You haven't heard the last of this.' She glared at Hannah. 'I'll report you to your superiors.'

'She will, too,' Hannah said as the double doors swept to behind her.

'Windbag,' Steve said. 'Mrs Morris, not you,' he hastened to add, his face softening into the suggestion of a smile. 'I didn't mean to be rude, only it's a long flight from Mexico and I'm short on sleep.'

'Is that where you've been?' A dreamy look came into Hannah's eyes as she imagined what it would be like to travel to such exciting places.

'I'm glad to be home and get some decent British weather,' he said, glancing towards the rain lashing the library window, 'after days of searing heat.'

'And exactly what is going on here?' another voice interrupted them.

Hannah sighed. Much more of this and she might as well hand in her notice and save Miss Lawrence the bother of making her redundant.

'Miss Lawrence.' Steve turned his charm on the new arrival. The chief librarian didn't look quite so pleased to see him.

'You're creating a disturbance, Mr Talbot, and I can't have that in my library.' Her eyes strayed to the polite notice on the wall requesting that conversation be kept to a minimum and conducted in a hushed voice.

'I do apologise for disrupting the peace and quiet,' Steve explained in a weary voice, 'but this is an emergency.'

'That's all very well,' Miss Lawrence replied, slightly mollified. 'I appreciate there are occasions when domestic crises arise, but Miss Lavender does have a job to do and you are preventing her from getting on with her work.'

'I merely wanted to know where her

mother is,' Steve pointed out. 'She has my house keys and I can't get in.'

'That seems a simple enough request. Hannah?' Miss Lawrence raised an eyebrow at her. 'Can you advise Mr Talbot of your mother's whereabouts?'

Hannah's glasses slipped down her nose. It was as if the library was holding its breath.

'I think she might be in America,' she admitted.

'Where?' Steve cracked back at her.

'She mentioned something about the Lone Star State.'

'That's Texas,' old Mr Matthews said as he joined the little group at the desk. 'My grandson worked there on a ranch one summer. Said it was the best work experience ever. He learned how to rein in a steer and he actually rode a bucking bronco at a rodeo. Nearly lost his teeth by all accounts.'

'Not now, Mr Matthews.' Miss Lawrence cast him a stern glance.

'No one 'cept Hannah ever listens to my stories these days,' he grumbled.

'She's a nice girl.' Mr Matthews tapped Steve on his arm. 'You ought to get together with her. That sister of hers is a bit much to take with all her protesting, but Hannah — she's different. Nothing's too much trouble.' Hannah squirmed as Jim Matthews fixed her with one of his steely stares. 'What's all this I hear about your mother taking off to get married to a Texan millionaire? Is it true?'

2

The smell of wood smoke misted the evening air. Giant gnats zigzagged in the twilight, promising a fine day tomorrow. Hannah ducked to avoid a shirt drying on a washing line strung across the branches of a tree. In the background someone was strumming a guitar and singing a romantic ballad in a pleasant baritone. Small groups sat round in semicircles, catching up with the chores of the day. Everyone smiled at Hannah and Lucy as the child tugged excitedly at her hand.

'Come on, Hannah, hurry up.'

Past experience had taught Hannah that whenever she visited her sister, sensible shoes were the order of the day. Carefully side-stepping the pools of mud caused by the earlier rain, she paced her strides to keep up with Lucy. Discarded banners had been carefully folded away under the trees and the atmosphere was one of calm and relaxation.

'Mummy,' Lucy squealed as she caught sight of the stunningly beautiful woman wearing a tatty denim skirt, green waistcoat and pink straw hat decorated with daffodils.

'Darling.' Ronnie opened her arms and scooped up her daughter and whirled her around. 'How's my favourite girl?'

Lucy giggled with delight. 'I drew a picture of you in art class today and Miss Maggs put it up on the wall.'

'Did she now? I'm impressed. I didn't know we had an artist in the family.'

'I called it 'Muddy Field' 'cause that's what you smell like.'

Ronnie's eyes met those of her sister's over her daughter's head. They exchanged a wry smile.

'Never think of being a diplomat, my darling.' Ronnie kissed her daughter's forehead.

'What's a diplomat?' Lucy asked.

'I'll tell you later.'

Ronnie, real name Veronica, had taken after their mother. Like Babs, her elder daughter was a free spirit. The moment she left school Ronnie had cast her hated hat into the hedge and vowed she was never going to wear beige again. Within weeks she had taken to travelling the countryside, embracing injustice. She was actually rather good at stating her cause, and local politicians had started to sit up and take notice of her views. Like her mother, Ronnie wasn't averse to using her looks to charm a crusty official round to her way of thinking or to get a news reporter to grant her media air time. When Lucy had been born six years ago, Hannah had hoped her sister might settle down to a more traditional lifestyle, but not even motherhood could quench Ronnie's roving ways.

'I can't give up, Han,' she explained. 'Can you see me living on an estate with respectable neighbours? I'd create coffee morning chaos. The residents' association would have me thrown out in seconds.'

Lucy's father was a drummer in a band and the marriage had by all accounts been lively. Hannah wasn't totally sure the ceremony they had attended under the stars was official, but Ronnie possessed a registrar's certificate proving there had been a marriage. After the band had moved on, Lucy's father had packed up his drums and gone with them. He reappeared on the scene from time to time and in his own way was devoted to his daughter, but like Ronnie he couldn't stay in one place for long.

Ronnie and Xan, short for Alexander, understood each other, and at times Hannah suspected they were happier apart than together. They both adored their daughter but neither could forsake their unconventional lifestyle. It had fallen to Hannah and her mother to provide Lucy with a more stable background and to make sure she went

18

to school and did her homework and didn't spend all her free time dancing under the night sky, as her mother was prone to do if the mood took her.

'Hi, Han,' Ronnie greeted her sister. 'You're late. I'd almost given up on you. You're looking pale. Something worrying you?'

Lucy scrambled free from her mother's arms. 'Can I explore?'

'Don't go near the river,' Ronnie called after her daughter as Lucy ran towards the group ranged around the campfire.

'We'll keep a good eye on her.' One of girls waved a greeting at Hannah. 'Fancy lentil stew and some fresh home-baked bread?'

Hannah sniffed the fragrant stew and realised she was seriously hungry. Her stomach had been too knotted up with tension for her to eat any lunch, and because of Lucy's tantrum at breakfast she had only managed to swallow a mouthful of toast.

'There you go.' The cook delivered two heaped plates of stew and a jug of apple juice. 'Enjoy.'

Ronnie settled down beside Hannah outside her small tent. 'Dig in. We'll talk later.'

'You're looking better already,' Ronnie said as Hannah cleared her plate. 'Sorry we haven't got any scones and cream for dessert. I know they're your favourite. There should be a good crop of blackberries in September, so you'll have to wait until then for some bramble jelly I'm afraid.'

'I couldn't eat another thing,' Hannah replied. She leaned back against a tree trunk and sighed with satisfaction. 'It's so peaceful here.'

In the distance she could hear the river meandering its course through the gentle Surrey countryside.

'It doesn't really get dark this time of year so you're seeing us at our best. It's not as cosy in the middle of winter when the ground's so frosty you think your feet are going to drop off, but you have to take the rough with the smooth.' Ronnie smiled. 'That's life.'

Despite their different characters, the two sisters were close. Both knew the other would be there for them no matter what.

A young girl collected their plates and took them down to the river to rinse.

'Sometimes I think it would be nice to do what you've done.'

'You'd be very welcome to join us. Sure I can't tempt you?'

'You know I can't do that.' Hannah was jerked back to reality with a jolt.

'Someone has to protect the environment for future generations, Han, otherwise the countryside will be one soulless block of concrete.'

'There's no need to start spouting your cause to me,' Hannah replied. 'You know I agree with all you're doing in principle.'

The sisters had had this conversation many times before. Hannah did what she could to help Ronnie by distributing leaflets and making sure her sister stuck to the letter of the law, but she was too peace-loving to take a more active part in the demonstrations. For that you needed someone with Ronnie's determination, and to her credit the small commune was run along very efficient lines. Somehow she had managed to sweet-talk a farmer into leasing them the land on the understanding they didn't harm any of his animals or indulge in antisocial activity, conditions Ronnie had been happy to accept.

'Sorry, Han. I know.' Ronnie smiled an apology. 'You and Mum are the only people who really understand me,' she said. 'I don't have to explain to you. You get what I'm all about.'

'We're family.'

'Talking of which, how is Mum?' Ronnie asked. 'I haven't seen her in ages.'

'That's because,' Hannah said, chewing her lip, 'you may as well know before Mrs Morris tells the whole town.'

'That old busybody. What's the fragrant Patti got wind of now?'

'I'm talking about Mum, actually.'

'Go on.'

'Steve Talbot came by the library today.'

'Don't get me started on him, Han.'

'He was looking for his house keys.'

'And?' Ronnie prompted. 'For goodness sake, Han, spit it out before sunrise.'

'I didn't have them.'

'I'd already worked that one out for myself. Mum's got them, hasn't she?'

'I presume so.'

'Then why didn't Steve ask her for them? He didn't need to come barging into the library, did he?' Ronnie grinned. 'Bet he disturbed the peace.'

'Mum wasn't at the house.' It was difficult to keep on topic when talking to Ronnie.

'She never is when he's away. Where's she gone this time?'

'She's having a little holiday.'

'Han, I really am running out of patience. What's all this to do with me, and where does Patti Morris fit into the plan of things?'

'She came back for her book. She'd

left it behind on the counter. To cut a long story short, she heard old Jim Matthews spilling the beans. I had no idea he knew.'

'Knew what? I really am going to have to shake you, Han, if you don't tell me.'

'She's got married again.'

'Mrs Morris has taken on a new husband? I don't believe it. No man could ever match up to her saintly Arthur.'

'Not Mrs Morris. Mum.'

'Mum's done what?' Ronnie shrieked.

'That's why she's not here. She's on her honeymoon.'

'Who with?'

'You remember Hal Beckett?'

'The one with the six-gallon hat and the Texan drawl?'

'That's the one.'

'And the huge ranch?'

'It was all very sudden and Mum wanted it kept secret.'

'How come you know if it's such a secret?'

'She had to tell someone.'

'So she chose you? That figures.'

'I've no idea how Jim Matthews found out.'

'If that isn't just like Mum.' Ronnie laughed. 'Well, good luck to her. Hal's a lovely man. Do you think we'll be able to rely on him for an input of funds every now and then?'

Both girls had liked the genial American who had endeared himself to Ronnie when he'd told her that in his youth he'd gone on anti-Vietnam rallies.

'Where are they going to live?' Ronnie asked.

'I don't know, but Steve wasn't exactly pleased by the news.'

'What's it got to do with him? Mum made it clear she was only a temporary housekeeper.'

'He's locked out of his house.'

A look of horror crossed Ronnie's face. 'I hope you didn't suggest he join us here? I mean I know we make everyone welcome, but there are limits. Besides, we haven't got a tent big enough for his ego.'

'I don't know why you've so taken against him.'

'I should have thought it was obvious, but if you'd like me to go into detail . . . '

Hannah shook her head.

'Well I can't help you I'm afraid. Like I said, it's been a while since I've seen Mum and she certainly wouldn't entrust me with her keys.'

'There's more,' Hannah said.

'We're not about to have a baby brother or sister, are we?' A smile tugged the corner of Ronnie's mouth. 'That would set tongues wagging.'

'No, it's not that.'

'What then?'

Hannah took a deep breath. 'I've lost my job.'

'What? Your poor lamb, why didn't you say?' Ronnie was now all concern.

'They're making cutbacks.'

'Yes, but why you? You're the best librarian they've got. You go the extra mile.'

'I'm also the newest employee. Miss

Lawrence told us all after work. We had to stay late, that's why I couldn't get here earlier.'

'How much notice did you get?'

'Effective immediately.'

'You mean like now?'

Hannah nodded.

'They can't do that. Want me to fight your case?'

'No,' Hannah pleaded. 'Don't do anything.'

'You could go to a tribunal.'

'What I'm trying to tell you is I'm not going to be able to look after Lucy full-time anymore, what with Mum away in America.'

'I wouldn't expect you to. Lucy can stay with me. Don't worry, there's a crèche with a proper matron. We are very organised. She'll be quite safe and I promise not to take her traipsing around the countryside if I get the call. There's always Etaine too, Xan's mother. So no worries on that score. What we really need to do is get you sorted. Now how can I help?'

'I've got a little bit of money put by.'

'You know there'll always be a place for you here,' Ronnie offered.

'Thanks, Ronnie. I appreciate the gesture.'

'But you prefer four walls and hot running water?'

Hannah nodded. 'But I don't think I'll be able to stay in my flat if I can't come up with the rent.'

'And you've nowhere else to go?' Ronnie asked. 'Any contacts in this library of yours?'

'They're mostly retired or students on grants or mothers with young children.'

'There's always Patti Morris.' Ronnie's eyes twinkled. 'She's got masses of room in that mansion of hers.'

'I'm not that desperate,' Hannah retaliated.

Another look of horror crossed Ronnie's face.

'Don't look now but I don't think we're done with the nasty shocks.'

Hannah sensed rather than felt a

presence behind her.

'We're full. So if you're looking for somewhere to spend the night you are out of luck. Try the farmhouse down the road. They do a nice bed and breakfast.'

Hannah knew from the tilt of Ronnie's chin that there was only one person in the world who could spark such a reaction from her.

'And how dare you accuse my sister of lying?'

'I did no such thing,' Steve Talbot spluttered.

'Yes you did. I hope you never find your keys,' Ronnie added for good measure, 'then you'll appreciate what it's like to be homeless.'

Hannah gulped as she looked from Ronnie to Steve. What had possessed him to visit the commune? Was he looking for a fight? The expression on his face as he glared at Ronnie suggested it was a possibility.

'Your mother eventually had the good grace to text me,' he admitted, 'to say she'd left the keys with my solicitor. She also informed me she would not be returning to Deneham in the foreseeable future.'

'Then why are you here?' Hannah demanded.

'I want you,' was the startling reply.

The ground lurched under Hannah as she felt the colour drain from her face. 'What for?' she managed to stutter.

'Your mother has broken her contract by leaving me in the lurch.'

'That's not Hannah's responsibility,' Ronnie interrupted.

'Now there I disagree with you. It is,' Steve insisted. 'Hannah witnessed the contract.'

Hannah frowned. She vaguely remembered signing a piece of paper. Neither she nor her mother had bothered to read it properly, but Steve had thrust it under their noses insisting they keep things on a business basis.

'What exactly did I agree to?' Hannah asked slowly.

'If your mother was unable to fulfil

all the terms and conditions of her contract, I am perfectly within my rights to ask you to take on her duties as housekeeper at Highworth House.'

Hannah opened her mouth to protest but Ronnie got in first.

'That's a terrific idea,' she enthused. 'Han's just lost her job in the library and she's about to be thrown out of her flat because she can't pay the rent.'

Steve nodded. 'Good. In that case I'll expect to see you some time tomorrow. We can firm up details then.'

With this parting shot, Steve turned away from the sisters and strode back the way he came.

3

Highworth House was a former vicarage and stood in the shadow of the church. Before the church had sold the property, Hannah had spent many happy afternoons working in the gardens as part of a school community project. The vicar's wife was a motherly woman, and she would make sure the girls took regular breaks; there was always a jug of refreshing home-made lemonade to hand after they had cleared away the overgrown brambles and weeded the rose beds.

Hannah and Ronnie had even slept over for a short while when their mother had taken off to Sicily as part of a vulcanologist team researching volcanoes and their effects on modern life. Quite how Babs fitted into the set-up Hannah never found out, but she hadn't minded. She got to stay in her beloved vicarage and over the summer she and Ronnie roamed the countryside, staying out all day, only coming home when driven by hunger. Hannah suspected that it was during that long, hot summer when Ronnie's love of the environment blossomed, and one night she confided her plans to her younger sister.

'You mean you're going to live in a tent?' A wide-eyed Hannah could hardly believe what she was hearing.

'I intend to set up a proper commune and live off the land,' Ronnie informed her.

'How are you going to do that?'

'I'm not sure yet, but I'll get there.' Ronnie spoke with all the conviction of youth.

When the vicar had retired and moved away, Highworth House had remained unoccupied for almost a year. The diocese had until then maintained the upkeep of the property, but with no incumbent it had been allowed to fall into disrepair. Hannah had been heartbroken to see the state of the old house, but after Steve Talbot had purchased it he had spared no expense. At first there had been a local reaction to an incomer buying the property, but opinion had softened after extensive renovation work had been carried out and Steve had allowed the summer fête to be held on his land. These days the vicarage was back to its former glory.

Hannah lingered on the front doorstep, inhaling the smell of the lavender bushes before pushing open the front door. The warm, woody smell of the polished floors greeted her. An agency had come in to clean after her mother's hurried departure and they had done a good job.

Hanging her coat on a hook in the vestibule, Hannah went through to the kitchen. Depositing her groceries on the pine table, she opened the window and breathed in the June air. The tended gardens were a riot of colour and the church wall at the back was covered with a bank of ivy. Hannah unlocked the kitchen door. The scent of honeysuckle rose to greet her like an old friend.

One of the vicar's more brutal gardeners had tried to uproot the honeysuckle, saying it got in the way, but the vicar's wife had stood her ground and Hannah was pleased that Steve, too, had allowed it to flourish.

'That is so brilliant,' Ronnie had repeated after Steve had departed the commune, her face alight with enthusiasm.

'What are you talking about?' Hannah stared at her sister. 'Steve Talbot is your worst enemy and you've just got me a job as his housekeeper.'

'Think about it, Han. With you in the camp, we'll have direct access to any of his plans.'

'What plans?'

Ronnie lowered her voice. 'Can you keep a secret?'

'No.' Hannah was firm. 'Whatever it is you know, I don't want to be a party to it.'

Ronnie carried on regardless. 'There's a story doing the rounds that one of the big conglomerates is planning to research the area looking for oil deposits.'

'In Deneham?' Hannah was aghast.

'We're not too sure exactly where, and it's no more than a rumour, but it's best to be on our guard.'

'How does Steve Talbot fit into this?'

'He's a geothermal engineer, isn't he?' Ronnie hedged.

'That's not the same thing.'

'It doesn't matter. He's got connections. These people all move in the same circles. He'll know something about it.'

'And you're saying you want me to spy on him?'

'I want you to keep your eyes and ears open.'

'I won't do it.' Hannah could be stubborn when she chose, and now was one of those occasions.

'Why not?'

'It's unethical.'

'I appreciate your scruples, Han, but do you want to see our skyline scarred with those nodding donkey things and the local wildlife decimated? The fields over the back are designated areas of outstanding natural beauty and if we have our way that's how they're going to stay. So are you in?'

Hannah chewed her lip. Yet again a member of her family was holding her to ransom. 'I still don't think it would be fair to pry on Steve,' she insisted.

'I'm not asking you to pry into his personal life,' Ronnie said, 'but can you live with the thought of contractors' vehicles trundling through Deneham, watching them carve up the country-side, knowing you'd done nothing about it?'

'Supposing you've got it wrong?'

'Then no harm done. Han?' Ronnie coaxed. 'Won't you even think about it?'

Hannah's lentil stewed churned in her stomach. The commune no longer seemed a haven of peace and tranquil-lity, and the storm lanterns created eerie shadows in the darkness as they swayed in the breeze. 'If I should find out anything in the course of my work that could be detrimental to Deneham,' she said slowly, 'then I'll let you know. Will that do?'

'Good girl.' Ronnie patted her sister on the back. 'Knew you'd come through.'

The campfire embers glowed in the encroaching twilight as the sun finally decided to slip down below the horizon and the sky turned a deep shade of crimson.

'I'd best be getting home. I've a lot to do.'

'I can't persuade you to stay over?'

'Lucy's got school in the morning,' Hannah replied. 'She'd better come back with me. We don't want her missing any lessons.'

'Where would I be without my sensible sister?' Ronnie kissed her cheek. 'Mum and I would be totally lost.'

'Mum's got Hal now. I wonder where she'll live?'

'Probably on that huge ranch of his. Doesn't he have an oil well or two about the place?'

'If he does you should hate him,' Hannah replied.

'There's a place for everything. Texas does oil wells. Deneham doesn't,' Ronnie affirmed.

A week later Hannah had given up her flat and moved into Highworth House. 'Do whatever you want. Make yourself at home,' Steve welcomed her at the door. He was wearing his trademark dark shirt and looked more relaxed than the last time they had met. He produced a bunch of flowers. 'For you,' he said, 'as a housewarming present. They're still dew-fresh. I picked them myself before my early-morning coffee.'

'You didn't have to do that,' Hannah insisted.

'Think of them as a bribe.'

Hannah stiffened. Surely in return for a few flowers he wasn't going to ask her to spy on Ronnie? She began to feel like a double agent.

'While I'm away you'll be responsible for the running of the house. I don't like to leave it unoccupied when I'm not here, but neither do I want too many people on the premises.'

'Sorry?' Hannah asked, confused.

'No parties, new age travellers or sisters on a mission, if you get my meaning?'

'Are you quite sure you want me to take up this post?' Hannah demanded, her earlier warmth towards him evaporating in an instant.

'Oh yes,' he agreed slowly, 'I want you.'

Hannah blushed, regretting her unfortunate choice of words. 'When are you off on your travels again?' She eyed his case by the door.

'I got a call just before you arrived. I'm not sure how long this tour will be but I'll see you when I get back.'

A taxi drew up as they were talking and Steve, grabbing up his travel bags, gave her a brief wave before striding towards the car.

Hannah was pleased to have time to herself to sort things out. She hoped that when Steve returned she would have established a household routine and be better placed to deal with his mood swings. There was something about them that was unsettling. She still wasn't absolutely sure if she had challenged him, whether or not he would have been able to legally enforce the clause in her mother's contract, but she had received no other offers of a job so she had little choice but to accept.

There wasn't much to do in the way of housework, but it was pleasant not to have to justify every moment of her working day to the eagle-eyed Miss Lawrence. Hannah doubted she would keep in touch with anyone from the library. Although she had enjoyed her time there, she had not made any lasting friends and one or two of her colleagues had talked about moving on, feeling it was only a matter of time before further cuts were made.

She did miss Lucy's company, however, and hoped that Ronnie would have a rethink about her letting her daughter come to live at Highworth

House. Steve had indicated that he had no objection to the child living there as long as Hannah had sole responsibility for her welfare. Whether or not this was a veiled reference to the invitation not being extended to her mother, Hannah wasn't too sure, but for the moment Lucy was staying with her mother.

Steve telephoned most days and Hannah passed on any messages, careful to keep the exchanges business-like. To date they had been nothing out of the ordinary and no news to excite Ronnie's interest.

Hannah turned on the radio and began to unpack her shopping. Sun streamed through the kitchen window and as one of her favourite singalongs came on the radio, she turned up the volume and began to gyrate to the music.

'Sorry to disturb you.'

Hannah shrieked and would have dropped her bag of sugar if it hadn't been for the quick reaction of the man at the back door. With lightning reflexes he leapt forward and caught it before the contents were spilled all over the floor.

'Best quarterback with the Traders there ever was,' he announced proudly as he deposited the rescued bag of sugar onto the kitchen table. 'Knew my catcher skills would come in useful one day.'

'Who are you?' Hannah gasped, 'and what are you doing here?'

'Sorry,' he apologised. 'I did try the front door but there was no answer, so I just followed the music. Jed Beckett at your service.' He sketched a bow. 'And whom do I have the honour of addressing?'

'My name's Hannah Lavender.'

'Then I guess we're brother and sister.'

Hannah clutched the back of one of the kitchen chairs. 'Did you say Beckett?'

'I did.'

'Are you anything to do with Hal Beckett?'

'He's my father, and as I understand it your mother is now married to him. I have to say I missed the ceremony. In fact I didn't know anything about it in advance.'

'Neither did we,' Hannah said.

'We?'

'Ronnie. She's my sister.'

'This is great. I now have two new sisters. Are there any more of you?'

'Ronnie has a daughter, Lucy.'

'That's fine. I'm not married but I do have two older sisters called Kylene and Jessica Mae. I don't see much of them. Kylene is a business lady and lives in New York, and Jessica Mae has lots of children and lives in Wisconsin.' He beamed at her.

'Do you know where Hal and my mother are?' Hannah asked, keeping her distance. Jed as looked as though he might envelop her in a bear hug.

'Last I heard, they were cruising the Caribbean. You haven't been in touch with your ma?'

Hannah shook her head. 'And you still haven't told me what you're doing here.'

'I came to look you up.'

'How did you know where to find me?'

'I got an email from Dad telling me he was married and that you worked in a library. I went there and met a scary lady called Ms Lawrence.'

Hannah nodded.

'She told me you now worked here as a housekeeper. Is that right?'

Again Hannah nodded.

'Dad said in his email if ever I was over here to schedule a visit, so here I am.'

'Do you work for your father?'

'I started off as a cowhand on the ranch. I didn't want to walk into a job he had created for me. I wanted to work my way up. Trouble was I got restless and one weekend I took off with the boys. Dad blew his top and we had a bit of a falling out.'

'What happened?'

'Somewhat foolishly, I told him I'd make my own way in the world. To cut a long story short, I haven't worked for him since. Is that coffee?' Jed looked at the jar on the table. 'I could sure use a mug. Why don't I fill the kettle?'

Glad to have something to do, Hannah put away the rest of the groceries while Jed sorted out the coffee.

'If you don't work for your father,' Hannah said, sitting down at the table, 'what do you do?'

'I'm a scout.'

'A what?'

'I know it sounds crazy, but I search out suitable areas for clients.'

'What sort of areas?'

'Anything they're looking for. It could be the location for a film, or somewhere new to go on vacation.'

'That sounds interesting.'

'Like all jobs it has its ups and downs, and the up is getting to meet my new sister.' Jed gave a lopsided grin. 'When do I get to meet Ronnie? She doesn't live with you?'

'Ronnie lives in the woods.' Hannah nudged a plate of biscuits towards Jed.

'Pardon me?' He almost choked on an oat flake. 'Did you say the woods?'

'She runs a commune.'

'Now that does sound my kind of thing. What does she do in this commune?'

'They weave, make bread, and they demonstrate.'

'You mean stuff like down with the bad guys?'

'That's right. Ronnie's off somewhere now doing her thing.'

'Then roll on Ronnie. I guess I'll have to delay my plans to meet up with her.'

'Where are you staying?'

'Does anyone rent out rooms in the area?'

'The local farmhouse does bed and breakfast.'

'That sounds just the thing. What say I book myself in, then come back and take you out to dinner? We need to get to know each other better.'

Hannah hesitated. Things were moving too quickly for comfort. 'I'm not sure,' she said. 'Why don't we wait until Ronnie gets back?'

'When will that be?' Jed looked disappointed.

'I don't really know,' Hannah admitted.

'I can show you the email from my father if you're worried I'm not who I say I am,' Jed offered. 'I have it right here.' He began searching the pocket of his leather jacket and eventually produced a crumpled sheet of paper. He flattened it out on the table. 'See, it's from Hal Beckett and signed 'Dad', and it's addressed to Jed. That's me. I've got my passport in my pocket if you want to take a look.'

Hannah began to laugh away her earlier fears. 'That won't be necessary.'

'Did I say something funny?'

'There's such a thing as too much information,' she said, 'and perhaps I did overreact a bit, but you gave me a shock.'

'I'm glad you're laughing. Does that mean dinner's back on the menu?'

'I suppose it does.'

Jed slid his hand across the table.

'Look out!' Hannah's warning came too late, as Jed knocked one of the coffee mugs onto the floor. It shattered to bits.

'Oh my goodness. I always was a clumsy coot.'

Hannah bent down to pick up the pieces just as Jed had the same idea. With a resounding crack they banged heads. Shrieking with shock, Hannah jerked back.

'What exactly is going on here?' an icy voice enquired from the doorway. Still trying to clear the tears from her eyes, Hannah looked up into the flinty greeny-amber eyes of a woman she had never before seen in her life.

4

'Harlequin, don't dawdle.'

Patricia Morris tugged at his lead. The dog obediently abandoned its investigation into the contents of the flowering tubs outside the library and trotted up the steps. 'Wait here and don't bark,' she instructed the crossbreed spaniel terrier as she attached his lead to one of the posts outside.

The library doors slid open and Mrs Morris sailed through and headed for the desk. 'Ah, Miss Lawrence, exactly the lady I wanted to see,' she greeted the chief librarian.

Miss Lawrence did not look quite so pleased with the prospective encounter but asked with a polite smile, 'What can I do for you?'

Patricia Morris inspected the area surrounding the desk. 'I understand Hannah Lavender no longer works here?'

'She doesn't. May I be of assistance?'

Patricia nodded in a satisfied manner. 'That sister of hers was a very bad influence. And as for the mother, the less said about her the better.'

'Quite. Now I believe you have been shown how to work the self-service checkouts?'

'I haven't come here to borrow a book,' Patricia tutted.

'What then?' Miss Lawrence asked.

'I've come here to register a complaint.'

'Against a member of staff?'

'Against that wretched commune.'

Miss Lawrence blinked behind her spectacles. 'I'm afraid you're not really in the right place to register an issue.'

'I don't want to register an issue. I want it closed down.'

'That's not something within our remit either.'

'Stop talking jargon at me, young woman, and tell me where to go.'

Miss Lawrence didn't know whether to look pleased at being addressed as a young woman, or concerned that the authorities might have a problem on their hands. 'I could give you the planning officer's details. He might be able to point you in the right direction.'

'I suppose it's a start,' Patricia admitted grudgingly.

'Why exactly do you want it closed down?' Miss Lawrence began tapping details onto her computer screen.

'It contravenes an ancient bye-law.'

'It does?'

'They are there without permission.'

'I think you'll find that's not true,' Miss Lawrence felt duty-bound to point out. 'The farmer has agreed to their use of the land. After that illegal rave last summer when some revellers cut through the wire and caused damage to his property, he's been worried about it happening again. He says having the official commune there acts as a guard dog and so far they have behaved in a responsible manner.'

Mrs Morris ignored the interruption. 'Goodness knows what they get up to after dark.'

'I wouldn't know about that,' Miss Lawrence gave in. There was no stopping Mrs Morris when she was on a roll, and she was clearly not in the mood to listen to reason.

'I can see their wretched tent thing from my spare bedroom window. They rarely retire before midnight.'

'Had your binoculars out again, have you, Patti?' Jim Matthews jabbed her in the ribs with an elbow. He cackled and winked at the chief librarian. 'I've heard she stands on the window sill to get a better view. Bet they're not half as interested in you as you are in them.'

'Please, Mr Matthews. How many times have I asked you not to call me Patti?'

'It's the name you was known by at school.' Jim Matthews unfortunately possessed a long memory and was a constant thorn in Patricia's flesh.

'I think this is the number you should contact.' Miss Lawrence came to Mrs Morris's aid as she passed over a slip of paper. 'If you are going down that

53

route, however, I would advise caution.'

'She's in the mood to stir up trouble.' Jim looked after her departing figure. 'And I call it a shame. It's not as if the commune does any harm.'

Miss Lawrence was an expert at keeping her views to herself. After years of working in a public library, she had learned to remain impassively neutral.

'Farmer Tony says they're no trouble, and they even helped when his cows broke out of their field,' Jim added. 'Rounded 'em all up in no time.'

'Hm.' Miss Lawrence made a non-committal noise at the back of her throat.

'So little Hannah's gone, has she?' Jim leaned on the desk.

'I am rather busy, Mr Matthews.' Miss Lawrence had no intention of engaging in dialogue with Jim Matthews, especially if he started asking questions about Hannah. Several of the regulars had expressed their views on her departure in no uncertain terms and Miss Lawrence had been forced to bear the brunt of their dissatisfaction.

'That's a shame. Think I might take a stroll up to the commune some time and have a word with her sister.' He tipped his hat. 'Tell her what's in the wind if Patti Morris gets her way. Forewarned is forearmed.'

Miss Lawrence sighed. The rumour she had heard but had not mentioned to Mrs Morris would have caused any concern she harboured over the commune's activities to pale into insignificance.

* * *

'Mr Talbot didn't tell me he had a fiancée.' Hannah stood her ground, determined she wasn't going to be intimidated by Alison Cooper.

Alison arched her finely plucked eyebrows. After Jed had made a hasty departure, promising to be in touch, Alison had rather grandly summoned Hannah to the study. 'We decided to keep it unofficial for the moment,' she admitted. Her silver ball necklace was dazzling Hannah. From where Alison was sitting behind the leather-topped desk, it was in direct sunlight and the rays caught the crystals.

'Why?' Hannah felt emboldened to ask.

Alison looked surprised by the question and a faint flush of colour stained the base of her neck.

'I don't feel that is any of your business, but if you must know our diaries are rather full. My media commitments can tie me up for months and Mr Talbot is never sure of his schedule. It would be very difficult to set a date to make an announcement.'

'Shall I tell Mr Talbot you're here the next time he telephones?' Hannah suggested.

The amber eyes turned a shade darker. 'That won't be necessary. I will take charge of the telephone from now on.'

'You're staying?' Hannah could hardly hide her dismay.

'I am, and I don't feel there's a need for the two of us to be here.'

It took Hannah a moment to absorb the full meaning of Alison's words. 'You mean you want me to leave?'

'I believe one of the terms of your employment was no permanent guests?'

'Jed isn't a guest and I didn't know he was going to drop by — and he certainly isn't staying. He's booking into Farmer Tony's bed and breakfast. And for your further information, Jed's father has just married my mother, and he was introducing himself to me, and Steve said I could have friends here if I wished.'

'Your personal life is none of my concern.' Alison dismissed her explanation with a wave of her hand. 'As far as I am concerned, you have broken the terms of your contract, and as such I am perfectly within my rights to dismiss you.'

Hannah's ears buzzed. 'No you're not. You didn't employ me. Mr Talbot did.'

'In his absence I have full authority to act on his behalf.'

Hannah blinked. 'Mr Talbot made no mention of you.'

'He's a busy man.'

'You're busy too, aren't you?' Hannah couldn't resist asking. 'How can you spare the time to answer his telephone with all your media commitments?'

The moment she spoke Hannah knew she had made an enemy of Alison Cooper.

'You have somewhere to go, I presume?' Alison asked in a cold voice.

Pride forbade Hannah from admitting she didn't. 'Mr Talbot employed me,' Hannah insisted stubbornly.

Indicating that the interview was at an end, Alison uncapped a fountain pen and opened her chequebook. 'I am well aware of your sister's strengths and I wouldn't want her suggesting you make a claim for unfair dismissal, so I am prepared to be generous.' She scrawled out a cheque and signed it with a flourish. 'That should more than cover things.'

Hannah glanced at the amount. It

was a generous sum, but one which she had no intention of accepting. In a gesture she knew she shouldn't have made and would probably regret, she carefully tore the slip of paper into little pieces, which she then threw in the air. The two women watched the bits of torn cheque float back down onto the table. With a bravado she was far from feeling, Hannah said, 'You haven't heard the last of this.'

Turning away to open the study door, Hannah didn't notice the shaft of uncertainty in Alison's amber eyes.

* * *

'She did what?' Ronnie demanded.

Hannah had been pleased to see her sister was back at the commune. She sank onto the waterproof covering the grass. 'Can I stay here?'

Ronnie dismissed her question with an airy wave of her hands. 'We've always got room for one more.'

'But not Steve Talbot?' Hannah

couldn't resist teasing Ronnie.

'After today I never want to see that man again. How dare he dismiss you?'

'He didn't, actually.'

'His representative did. That amounts to the same thing.' Ronnie thrust a mug of herbal tea into her sister's hands. 'What I suggest we do is — ' she began.

'Nothing,' Hannah stopped her.

'What?' Ronnie was scandalised. 'Steve Talbot has infringed your human rights.'

'Maybe he has, and maybe he hasn't, but I want to move on with my life. You've got better things to do than worry about me.'

'Han, I'm your sister. It's my job description to worry about you. You're so sweet and nice, people take advantage of you. It's up to me to make sure you don't get squashed into the ground.'

Hannah grinned at her sister. 'Up the revolution,' she said.

'All right, I'll take a back seat,' Ronnie agreed, 'but if things turn nasty you know where to come. Now tell me about Jed,' she said.

'He turned up out of the blue,' Hannah said. 'You'd like him. He's staying at Tony's farmhouse for a few days and he's offered to take us out for dinner.'

'Does he know I'm vegetarian?' Ronnie demanded.

'We didn't get around to discussing diets,' Hannah replied. 'After Alison descended on us he made a hasty exit but he said he'd be in touch.'

'In that case we'll take a walk down to the farmhouse later and have a word with him. What does this Jed do, by the way?'

'He said he was a scout.'

'Isn't he a little old for shorts and singing songs around a campfire?' Ronnie asked.

'Not that sort of scout. He looks for things. Ask him to tell you all about it when we meet up.'

'Hannah!' There was a loud squeal behind her before Lucy hurled herself into her aunt's arms.

'Good news, sweetheart,' Ronnie said. 'Han's coming to stay.'

'Yay!' Lucy executed a war dance. 'That means I can have real sausages for tea.'

Ronnie put her hands on her hips and sighed with mock indignation. 'Have you been feeding meat to my daughter?' she demanded of her sister.

'Not every day,' Hannah assured her, 'and as I haven't got any sausages on me at the moment, we're going to have to do without tonight.'

Lucy made a face. 'Lettuce and seeds. Yuck. I'm going to see the baby ducks.' She raced off.

'You are getting my girl into bad ways, and as a penance you can peel the carrots for the soup. Then while it's simmering, what say we take a stroll up to the farmhouse? Hannah? What's the matter?'

'That car,' she said, looking over her shoulder.

'What about it?'

'It can't be.' She shook her head.

'Can't be what?'

'It looked very like Steve's four-by-four.'

'Probably his lady friend marking her territory.'

'That must be it,' Hannah agreed. 'Now where are these carrots you were talking about?'

5

The early sunlight filtered through the gaps in the tent flaps. Hannah's back ached and her eyes were gritty from a disturbed sleep. Lucy stirred on the camp bed next to her, her brown curls sticking out from her sleeping bag.

Hannah wriggled uncomfortably as she gradually remembered all that had happened the day before. This situation could not continue. She and Lucy had to find somewhere permanent to live. Despite Ronnie's assurances that Lucy would be well cared for, this was no life for a child. Lucy might find it exciting for a little while, but the child had been used to a proper bed, a bathroom and a regular routine — as had Hannah.

Hannah tried to squint at her watch. She had no idea of the time but something had woken her. She tensed, sensing shadows on the canvas. Someone was moving about outside the tent.

'Ronnie,' she said, jabbing her sister in the ribs.

'Wassat?' Ronnie mumbled.

'We've got an intruder.'

'It's probably a cow nosing around. Go back to sleep.'

'Hello? Anyone awake?' a male voice enquired.

Hannah shrieked.

'Who's there?' Ronnie called out.

'Only me, Farmer Tony. Sorry to wake you so early.'

Ronnie undid the tent flap and poked her head through the gap. 'Have the cows got out again?'

'I've got to move you on.'

'What? Why?'

'I'm contravening a bye-law by allowing you to use my land for non-farming purposes. If I'm caught I think I'll be in for a huge fine, and my finances aren't up to it.'

'That's ridiculous,' Ronnie objected. 'Why's no one raised the matter before?'

'I don't know.'

'We haven't been given official notice to leave.'

'I've heard you're about to be served with a notice to quit, so I thought I'd warn you before things turned nasty.'

'What's going on?' Hannah whispered, anxious not to wake Lucy.

'We've got trouble.'

'Someone logged an objection,' Tony said. 'Jim Matthews alerted me. My wife says you'd be very welcome at the farmhouse.'

'Thanks, Tony.' Ronnie smiled. 'But there are too many of us. We couldn't possibly impose on you. How long have we got?'

'It's difficult to say. I feel so bad about it. I can't get my head around anything.'

'It wasn't your fault, Tony,' Ronnie reassured him. 'I'll wake the others and we'll have a council meeting.'

'You've got my mobile number if you need me. I'll be in the top field. Cows need milking no matter what.' He stomped off.

'What are we going to do?' Hannah

asked. Ronnie was already wriggling into her clothes.

'Don't look so worried. This isn't the first time this sort of thing has happened.'

'It's never happened to me before.'

'It'll all sort itself out in the end, you see.' Ronnie hugged her sister. 'Can I ask you to keep an eye on Lucy?'

'Who do you think complained about us?' Hannah asked.

'Didn't you say you thought you saw Steve's four-by-four racing past yesterday?'

'He can't be involved. He's not in the country.'

'His girlfriend is, and from what you told me about her it sounds the sort of thing she might do. Talk later.' With this parting shot Ronnie was gone.

'Aunty Hannah?' Lucy murmured.

Realising this was no time to fall apart, she smiled brightly at her niece. 'Time to get up,' she announced.

'It's awfully early.'

'We're going on a big adventure. Why don't you pack up your things?'

'What about breakfast?' Lucy's brown eyes were wide with excitement.

'I'll see what I can find. Promise me you'll stay here if I take a look outside?'

'Promise,' Lucy giggled. 'This is fun.'

Thrusting her feet into a pair of boots and shrugging on a holey jumper, Hannah scrambled outside. People were beginning to stir as Ronnie began doing the rounds and explaining what was going on.

'Hannah,' a voice called out behind her.

'Jed,' she greeted him with surprise.

'Tony's wife just broke the news. Is there anything I can do?'

Their meeting at the farmhouse the previous evening had been a great success. Ronnie and Jed got on together well and had exchanged stories about their successful demonstrations and sit-ins.

'Ronnie is trying to organise something,' Hannah informed him. 'It's all a bit of a muddle at the moment.'

'Have you got anywhere to go?'

'Not right now.' Hannah refused to

panic as she explained, 'Tony wasn't sure when the authorities would arrive, but it sounded official.'

'I hate hanging around like a spare part. There must be something I can do.'

'Have a word with Ronnie. I've got to look after Lucy.'

'Sure.' Jed flicked a hand to her cheek. 'We'll pull through.'

Hannah didn't share Ronnie and Jed's optimism, but everyone else seemed to be getting on with the tasks in hand with quiet efficiency. Hot water had already been boiled and Hannah managed to make two mugs of tea and a sandwich for Lucy's breakfast.

She staggered back to the tent. Ronnie's boots were too big for her and she could feel them slipping off her feet. Lucy had looped back the tent flap and begun to tidy up.

'Good girl,' Hannah praised her. 'Here's your breakfast.'

Lucy squatted down on her sleeping bag and began to munch contentedly.

Hannah perched on one of the logs and sipped her tea. The sun was warm on her back and it was promising to be a fine day.

'Would you like some sandwich, Hannah?' Lucy asked. 'You're not eating anything.'

Hannah managed to raise a smile. The thought of food choked her. 'I'll have something later,' she said.

'I haven't cleaned my teeth,' Lucy confessed. 'Will it matter?'

'We'll do that later too,' Hannah said. 'Hurry up and get dressed.'

'You do look funny in that red jumper,' Lucy sniggered. 'Your hair's all spiky like a smelly old scarecrow.'

'Well thank you for the compliment.' Hannah raised her arms in a parody of a scarecrow, making Lucy squeal.

A figure emerged from behind the tent. Stifling a shriek of her own, Hannah found she was looking into the angry eyes of Steve Talbot. 'Where did you come from?' she demanded.

Steve looked her up and down, his

eyes taking in every detail of her appearance. 'Lucy's right. You look like a tramp.'

'If I do it's because of you.' Hannah experienced an uncharacteristic urge to fling what remained of her tea at Steve, but with Lucy watching she managed to restrain herself.

'What have I done now?' he demanded.

'If you hadn't dismissed me I wouldn't be sitting here looking like a tramp.'

'I did no such thing. I've just got back from my latest trip and yet again I find I am locked out of my house. What is it with your family?'

'My family?' Hannah squawked in outrage, 'What about your fiancée?'

'My what?'

'Alison Cooper.'

'We are not engaged.'

'Whatever. She said I had breached the terms of my employment and since that seems to be something you know all about, I didn't hang around to catch the full details.'

'What exactly did you do this time?' Steve enquired.

'I was entertaining a guest who happened to call by unexpectedly. All we were doing was sharing a coffee in the kitchen.'

'I don't believe you.'

'Please yourself,' Hannah replied. 'I have better things to do than stand around in a muddy field listening to you accusing me of being a liar, so if you'll excuse me.' Her boots slipped, causing her to lose her footing. Steve grabbed her arm.

'Not so fast.'

'Mummy,' Lucy shouted at the top of her voice, 'there's a man attacking Hannah!'

Within moments an angry crowd surrounded them. 'What's going on?' one of the women demanded.

'We've every right to be here, so you can unhand Hannah,' another put in.

'Shame on you,' a third murmured, 'attacking a defenceless woman. You officials are all the same.'

'Police brutality!' The cry was taken up.

'I am not an official,' Steve protested, dropping his hold on Hannah's arm. 'Neither am I with the police.'

'Then state your business.' A bearded man stepped forward.

'I can tell you exactly what he's doing here,' a clear voice broke out behind them. Everyone turned to look as Ronnie strode into the centre of the action. 'This, ladies and gentlemen, is Steve Talbot, the person responsible for reporting us to the authorities.'

'Now hold on one moment,' Steve blustered.

'Are you the one who sacked Hannah?' someone else asked.

'He's that as well.'

'All I want is the keys to my house.'

'You was spoutin' the same story last week in the library,' Jim Matthews ambled over. 'Haven't you found 'em yet?' His weathered face broke into a smile. 'Wouldn't make much of a detective, would you?'

'At the risk of being rude, butt out, Jim, there's a good man,' Steve said.

'Before you get around to being rude,

you'd better hear what I've got to say,' Jim replied. 'Sorry to break up the party, folks, but Steve here isn't responsible for reporting you.'

'Then who is?' Ronnie demanded.

'Not my place to say.' Jim pursed his mouth. 'But I came to tell you there's room for the little 'uns down the health centre for those that's got nowhere to go. I've been talking to one of the nurses and she's coming in especially early to see to things.'

'Jim,' Ronnie beamed at him, 'you are an angel. And that's more than can be said for you,' she added, glaring at Steve, 'and don't you dare start spouting contracts at me again. I'm not in the mood.'

'I've come to offer Hannah her job back.'

'Then what are you doing standing around here? Hannah, off you go, and take Steve with you.'

'I can't get into my house,' Steve protested. 'My keys are missing.'

'Not that old chestnut.' Like Jim,

Ronnie displayed little sympathy for his predicament.

'These them?' Jed Beckett dangled a key fob in front of Steve.

'Yes they are, and who are you?'

'Meet the cause of all the trouble. Jed Beckett at your service.' He sketched a bow. 'I was the unwelcome visitor Hannah was entertaining. I promise I didn't make off with the teaspoons. You can count them when you get back.'

'What are you doing with my keys?'

'Your lady friend left them with Farmer Tony before she left for London. I brought them down here this morning for Hannah to use to get back into your house. She told me she left some of her things behind.' A wary look entered Jed's eyes. 'You're not going to start accusing us of intent to break and enter, are you?'

'Just let him try,' Ronnie interrupted. 'I'm up to speed when it comes to this sort of thing.'

'Stop casting me as the villain of the piece,' Steve protested.

'I wouldn't if you didn't wear the

uniform so well,' Ronnie responded.

'Stop it, you two.' Hannah thrust herself between them then hurriedly stepped back. Although Steve was wearing a denim fleece, she could feel the heat from his body and it was an unsettling experience. As if sensing her unease, Steve turned away.

'I'm still not clear who you are.' He looked at Jed. 'But thank you for these.'

'Don't mention it,' was the affable reply.

'Why are there so many people on this site?' Steve asked.

'We are being moved on, as if you didn't know,' Ronnie replied. 'If you give me your word it wasn't you who reported us, then I'd like to know who it was.'

'We haven't got time to go into all that now, Ronnie,' Hannah reminded her. 'Did you mean what you said about offering me my job back?' she asked Steve.

'Maybe you should take up the offer,' Ronnie murmured in her sister's ear. 'Remember our deal?'

'Because if you did, it's got to be on my terms,' Hannah insisted, raising her voice in an attempt to drown out Ronnie's remark about snooping.

'You're hardly in a position to bargain.' Steve looked slightly taken aback.

'What about Alison Cooper?'

'She acted totally outside her authority,' Steve replied.

'What about me?' a small voice blurted out, and Hannah felt a warm hand slip into hers. 'I'm Lucy.' She smiled up at Steve.

He looked down at the child. 'If your mother agrees, you'd be most welcome to stay with your aunt,' he explained in a kinder voice.

'Ronnie,' Hannah appealed to her sister, 'I think it would be for the best if Lucy came with me. I mean, I know you said you'd only let her live in Highworth House over your dead body?'

'I said no such thing,' Ronnie blustered. It was the first time in her life that Hannah had seen her sister lost for words.

'I, too, seem to recall you saying something along those lines, I have to admit,' Steve added with the suggestion of a smile.

'I may have expressed my views but I'm sure I didn't put them quite like that.' Ronnie was now rather red in the face.

'Lucy has to stay somewhere, Ronnie, and until you're sorted out it would be the best solution.'

'Would I be welcome to visit my daughter?' Ronnie challenged Steve.

'I can't really refuse you visiting rights, can I?' Steve answered courteously.

'What about this lady friend of yours?' Ronnie demanded. 'She seems rather keen on ejecting people from your premises.'

Steve paused then said, 'I have a feeling in your particular instance if Alison tried to eject you from the premises her efforts might not meet with success.'

Before Ronnie could reply, the quiet of the morning was shattered by the background throb of motorbike engines.

Moments later a posse of high-powered bikes roared into the compound and ground to a halt. Exhaust fumes curled on the morning air and leather saddles creaked as the bikers dismounted.

'Xan?' Ronnie looked uncertainly at one of the bikers.

'Daddy!' Lucy squealed and ran towards him.

He removed his helmet, revealing a shock of bushy hair, and beamed at his daughter.

'Hello, darling,' he said. 'Pleased to see me?'

6

The return to Highworth House was made easier with Lucy's constant chattering in the back seat of the car. 'Have you got any animals, Mr Talbot?' was the first question.

'I travel too much to keep a pet,' he replied.

'I like rabbits and dogs and ducks,' she said. 'Hannah, can I have a guinea pig if I promise to feed it and change its water?'

'You can't have one right now,' Hannah replied. 'You're Mr Talbot's guest, remember.'

'Mr Talbot,' Lucy began.

'You can call me Steve,' he said.

'Are you sure?' Hannah intervened.

'Makes me think of my father when people call me Mr Talbot. He came from a generation when nobody ever used first names unless they were family.'

'What did he do?'

'He was an engineer. He loved anything mechanical.'

'My daddy's got a motorbike,' Lucy piped up.

'I saw him,' Steve replied.

After Xan had been apprised of the reason why everyone was leaving the commune, he and his fellow bikers had set to helping the settlement dismantle, and to Hannah's surprise the task was completed quickly and efficiently. Everyone, it seemed, had a contingency plan for this type of situation.

'It's a hazard of the job,' Ronnie explained to a bemused Hannah.

'I'd hardly call protesting a job,' Hannah pointed out.

'We work too, you know,' Ronnie said with her gentle smile, 'but I'm not about to argue with you on that one, little sister; I've too much to do. Now, Lucy Lockett,' she said, turning to her daughter, 'are you sure you've got everything?' She inspected the array of boxes Steve was loading into his car.

'I've packed my toy rabbit and my books, and Hannah helped with my clothes.'

'Then give me a kiss.'

'Where are you going, Mummy?' Lucy asked.

'Daddy and I are going off on a little holiday to see if we can find somewhere new to live, but we'll be back sooner than you know. And when we are, I want to hear about all the exciting things you've been up to.'

Xan hugged his daughter. 'You be a good girl for your aunty Hannah now, you hear?'

'Will you bring me a present?' Lucy asked her father.

'I'll think about it.'

Xan and Ronnie had waved at them as Steve had joined the convoy snaking out of the field back onto the road leading down from the farm.

'Is Xan his real name?' Steve asked as they drove along.

'It's short for Alexander. He'd strangle me for telling you this, but he calls himself Xan Power, though his real name is Alexander Pugh.'

'We all have our secrets.' Steve smiled.

'What's yours?' Lucy demanded from the back seat.

Hannah cast him a tolerant glance. 'You don't have to answer,' she mouthed at him.

'I'm a really nice guy,' he said to Lucy, 'despite what your mother thinks of me. Now you have to tell me your secret in exchange.'

'You won't tell?' the little girl asked, a fearful look on her face.

'We promise,' Hannah smiled.

'I quite like Hannah's proper sausages, not Mummy's vegetarian ones.'

'That is a big secret to keep.' Steve winked at Hannah. 'Your turn.'

'Do I have to?' Hannah wished it wasn't so easy to like Steve. Her perception of him had been coloured by Ronnie's opinion of geothermal engineers, but Steve could be warm-hearted, kind and funny when he wasn't being dogmatic. Hannah couldn't imagine him doing anything to damage the planet.

'I know what your secret is,' Lucy crowed.

Hannah swivelled around. 'You do?'

'You like reading the latest busters from the library.'

'The latest what?' Steve frowned.

'She means blockbusters,' Hannah admitted.

'Not those lurid things old Patti Morris reads?'

'I suppose ex-librarians are supposed to have loftier tastes,' Hannah replied, 'but I've always found big words difficult to understand, and the classics are full of long passages and pages of descriptions.' She tilted her chin. 'So, there you have it.' Her brown eyes flashed dangerously, as if daring him to make something of it.

'I like the sports mags,' Steve admitted. 'You sometimes need a break from the intensity of ecological issues. Like the classics, they can be a bit dusty at times.'

'You're beginning to sound like Ronnie.'

'She and I aren't all that different. She just goes about things in an alternative way.'

'You mean she makes more of a fuss?'

'I wouldn't put it quite like that, but I'm all for renewable energy and I believe in using natural resources to get it. Did you know people have used under-floor heating for years? The ancient Romans used it in their spa baths, and we can go back even further than that. There's evidence the Chinese built a palace around a stone pool as far back as the third century B.C. So you see, there's nothing new in green issues.'

'Why, then, has Ronnie taken against you?' Hannah asked.

'Did she study much at school?' Steve asked.

'She couldn't wait to leave.'

'It's often the case. I'd like to tell her exactly what I do and explain we're of similar minds, but I don't think she would listen to the likes of me. She's active and I'm more hands-on.'

'She and Xan are activists. They met at a rally.'

'They didn't stay together?'

'They're happier living apart and Lucy is their main concern.'

'She certainly loves both her parents.'

'Xan's a good father for all his wandering ways. He gets that gene from his gypsy mother. She lives in a caravan in the woods.'

'What about Mr Pugh, his father?'

'He married Etaine against his family's wishes. They were very middle-class. I don't know what happened to him. So there you have all the family skeletons out of the closet — at least I think that's all of them.'

Their conversation was conducted in low voices. Exhausted by the early start to the day, Lucy had fallen asleep in the back seat.

'But you're the one who provides Lucy with sausages and a clean bed for the night?'

'Sometimes Ronnie gets carried away with her causes. She'd take Lucy with her on more protest marches if I didn't stop her.'

'It's difficult to believe the pair of you are sisters.'

Hannah was saved from replying as they drew into the forecourt of Highworth House.

'Here we are then. Home.'

'Can I explore the garden, Hannah?' Lucy yawned and rubbed at her eyes.

'Is that all right with you, Steve?'

'She'll be quite safe,' he replied. 'There's no pond or anything like that for her to fall into.'

'Ten minutes, that's all,' Hannah said, 'and don't leave the garden.'

'I promise.' Lucy scampered off and Steve began unloading their stuff from the back of the vehicle.

'I'll ask the gardener to store the site things in one of the outhouses,' he said. 'For the moment most of it can stay under the car port.' He picked up some painted banners and with a wry smile as he read the robust slogans, he stowed them by the side of the garage.

'I didn't realise there would be quite so much,' Hannah apologised.

'I expect poor old Farmer Tony got more than his fair share of trappings too.' Steve straightened his back. 'There, that's the lot. Let's go inside, shall we? Can't wait to see the old place again.'

'Do you know how long you'll be at home this time?' Hannah asked as Steve unlocked the door.

'I've no idea. I never do know, but I hope it'll be slightly longer than a week.'

'And Miss Cooper?'

'Alison? What about her?'

'When will she be back?'

'She lives in London during the week. When she comes down here she rents a room in a large country house. Alison and I lead largely separate lives. She's no more than a friend really, but I don't think she sees the relationship as platonic.'

'I wasn't — ' Hannah paused, uncertain how to go on. ' — being nosey.'

'No matter,' Steve said, dismissing

her explanation. 'You had to know. But remember one thing — I run my own house. Alison is only a guest here. She had no right to act as she did in asking you to leave.'

'And you're not engaged?'

'Neither officially nor unofficially.' Steve went back to the car and staggered into the kitchen with a box of Lucy's things. 'That's about everything. You can sort out Lucy's accommodation later. Take any of the rooms on the first floor. They've all been recently decorated. I've got the rooms over the stable block, so we won't get in each other's way. Now, was there anything else?'

'Actually there was,' Hannah began.

'Yes?' Steve asked slowly.

'Jed Beckett.'

'This new brother of yours? What about him?'

'Is he free to visit?'

'Any time he likes. Ronnie and Xan can come too, but I draw the line at using my premises for protesting.'

'They won't do anything like that,'

Hannah assured him, 'and thank you.'

'What for?'

'Everything.' Hannah blushed. 'I'm not like Ronnie. I don't really enjoy living on the wild side.'

'I'd hardly say she did that.'

'You know what I mean. She takes after our mother.'

'And your father?'

'He was a gas-meter reader. He loved books so I suppose I take after him.'

'I'm sorry you lost your job in the library,' Steve said.

Hannah was surprised to realise she hadn't thought about her old job for a while and that she wasn't missing the work as much as she thought she would. 'Ronnie would say it's an opportunity to develop.'

'She could be right. Now, back to practicalities. If you fancy some coffee I'd love a cup — black, no sugar. I'll be in the study downloading my latest notes and catching up on paperwork.' He paused in the doorway. 'Oh, and Hannah?'

'Yes?' she looked up from filling the kettle.

'Your first job is to get some spare house keys cut. I can't face being locked out again.' The sunlight caught the fob as Steve dropped the keys on the kitchen table. In the distance the telephone began to ring. 'You can answer that. If it's someone from Peru demanding my urgent presence tell them I'm out,' Steve said.

The call wasn't from Peru.

'Hello, is that you, Hannah?' an uncertain voice enquired.

'Miss Lawrence?'

'Yes, it's me,' the chief librarian said with the suggestion of a nervous laugh. 'I wasn't sure if I'd got the right number. I had a bit of trouble tracking you down.'

'What can I do for you?' Hannah asked.

'The thing is, well . . . Look, would you mind if I came to visit you? There's something I need to get off my chest.'

7

'I plan on working in the library for most of the morning,' Steve announced the next day after breakfast, 'so unless it's an emergency I don't want to be disturbed.'

'Someone from the library will be coming for coffee, if that's all right?' Hannah asked as she cleared the table. 'I thought we could use the conservatory. It's nice and sunny there and I can keep an eye on Lucy.'

'You're not thinking of going back to your old job?' Steve was quick to ask, a frown creasing his forehead. 'I don't have to remind you of the terms of your contract?'

'While we're on the subject I would actually like to have a copy of that contract my mother and I signed,' Hannah clipped back her reply. 'She didn't leave one with me.'

'You don't need to see it right now, do you?' Steve asked.

Hannah was determined to stand her ground. 'As you keep quoting terms and conditions at me, I'd like to know what I'm talking about.'

'Who's coming to see you this morning?' Steve changed the subject, 'and why?'

Hannah's minor victory felt hollow as she replied, 'I don't know why she wants to see me. It's Miss Lawrence.'

'Tell her you're spoken for if she suggests re-employment.'

Without Ronnie's presence creating a shadow between them, Hannah found working for Steve more relaxed despite their occasional spats about why he could never find a matching pair of socks and the state of his shirts, for which Hannah insisted she wasn't responsible; and if he wanted a decent shirt, then he could always go out and buy one.

Lucy was happy exploring her new home and was now in the garden digging the patch of earth Hannah said she could use to grow vegetables. They'd bought a little packet of seeds in town when they'd gone to get the new keys cut, and Lucy was busy digging a small trench in which to plant her radishes and carrots.

'Am I not to get any peace?' Steve muttered as the telephone began ringing again. He disappeared to answer it, leaving Hannah to her housekeeping duties.

Miss Lawrence was punctual and to Hannah's surprise kissed her on the cheek. 'It's lovely to see you, dear.' She handed over a bunch of flowers. 'Only garage forecourt, I'm afraid, but they looked very fresh, although — ' She glanced out of the window. ' — you do seem to have a garden full of better blooms.'

'Hello, Miss Lawrence. Thank you for the flowers. It's the thought that counts. I'll put them in water.'

'You must call me Val,' the older woman insisted. 'No need to be so formal now I'm no longer your superior. How are you settling in, working for Mr Talbot?' she asked.

'Very well.'

'It played on my conscience when you were dismissed, but I hope you understand it wasn't my decision.'

'Ronnie always says these things happen for a reason.' Hannah finished filling the vase and placed the flowers on the window ledge, then carried the tray of coffee and biscuits through to the conservatory.

'This is lovely.' Miss Lawrence settled down in one of the wicker chairs. She looked around at her surroundings with an appreciative smile. Lucy waved to them from the garden. Miss Lawrence waved back. 'Your niece is with you here permanently, is she?' she asked.

Hannah poured the coffee and nudged a plate of biscuits in Miss Lawrence's direction. 'For the moment.'

'A much better arrangement. Perhaps things will settle down for a bit now.'

'Did you hear about the commune being closed down?'

'I was sorry about that. It all happened so suddenly. I presume your sister isn't staying at Highworth House? She and Mr Talbot don't exactly hit it off, do they?'

'Ronnie's husband turned up the morning we received the news about the intended eviction. He and Ronnie went off together somewhere to try and sort something out. I was very surprised at how well organised the transfer was. Apparently they were contravening a bye-law that the farmer knew nothing about.'

'Well I am glad you're suitably settled. I didn't like the idea of you camping in a field.'

'What exactly did you want to see me about, er, Val?' Hannah asked, feeling a little awkward addressing her former boss by her first name.

'It's difficult to know where to start, and I've no wish to break any confidences. I came to you because I don't know where your sister is.'

'Neither do I at the moment, but she

will be back soon. She's doesn't like being parted from Lucy longer than necessary, and Xan is a responsible father too.'

'When he's not roaring around the countryside on that monster of a motorbike.' Val didn't look convinced.

Hannah waited for Val to go on, wondering when she would get down to the real reason for her visit.

'As you know,' she began, 'working in the library you hear all sorts of gossip. I try not to listen, but sometimes you can't help it. People don't exactly keep their voices down.'

'Go on,' Hannah urged.

'There have been lots of meetings about the cutbacks and — ' Val coloured. ' — I wasn't eavesdropping, but I couldn't help overhearing something I probably wasn't meant to. I'd been to a meeting myself and I was on the way back to the library. An office door was open, you see, and two of the planning people were discussing development in the area. They didn't realise

I was in the corridor. Anyway, one of them said he would be pleased to read the report on the drilling research.'

'Drilling research?' Hannah frowned in puzzlement. 'Where?'

'I don't know, exactly, and you must remember this is only what I overheard, but it would have been the sort of thing Ronnie would have taken up, wouldn't it?'

'You don't have any more details?'

'None at all. I believe the company concerned were talking about — what was the word they used? Not a rep.' She clicked her fingers. 'A scout, that was it. They were employing a scout and he was going to see what he could find out on an unofficial basis.'

'Did you say scout?' Hannah sat up straight.

'Yes. Strange word, wasn't it? I suppose it's nothing to do with Mr Talbot?'

Hannah shook her head. 'No, not Steve, but I think I know who it might be.'

'You do?'

An image of Jed's smiling face flashed through Hannah's mind's eye.

Val looked over her shoulder as if she feared being overheard, then leaned forward and lowered her voice. 'A word of warning, dear. It was only hearsay, and I'm not even sure I got my facts right, so it would be best to tread carefully. But we really don't want our countryside interfered with more than necessary, do we? It's not often I find myself onside with your sister's activities, but on this occasion I can sympathise.'

'Do you think that was why the commune was closed down? With the protesters out of the way it would be much easier to carry out any research without being spied on, wouldn't it?'

'Oh dear.' Val bit her lip in a distressed manner.

'What is it? What's the matter?' Hannah asked.

'I fear it was an unfortunate coincidence.'

'Do you know something else you're not telling me?' Hannah demanded.

'In strictest confidence?' Val's face was screwed up as if she were in pain.

A tap on the window interrupted them.

'Hannah,' Lucy pleaded, 'I'm thirsty. Can I please have a glass of orange juice?'

Stifling her irritation at being interrupted at such a crucial point, Hannah went to fetch the jug from the kitchen. She discovered Steve lurking by the fridge.

'How's the coffee morning going?' he asked.

'Fine.' Hannah did her best to keep her voice steady. 'Can I get you anything?'

'I was looking for a cup of coffee but don't concern yourself, I'll make my own.' He flicked the switch on the jug kettle. 'You can go back to your friend. I know how to boil water.'

'Steve.' Hannah took a deep breath. 'What?'

'You don't know anything about research in this area?'

'What sort of research?'

'I don't know really.' Hannah shook her head. 'It's probably nothing. Forget I mentioned it.'

'Is this something to do with your sister?' he demanded with a frown.

'It was something I heard, that's all.'

'If I can be of any help you only have to ask. I keep a low profile because I know how some of the locals feel about me, but my work takes me away to other countries. I do nothing on a local scale.'

Ashamed of her suspicions, Hannah picked up Lucy's orange juice and made her way back into the conservatory.

'You were a long time,' Val said. 'Lucy and I were about to come looking for you.'

'Mr Talbot was making some coffee,' Hannah explained. 'Here you are, Lucy.'

'Can I take it outside?' she asked.

'As long as you don't spill anything.'

'I won't.' Carefully carrying the paper cup between her hands, Lucy made her way back down the steps and onto the lawn.

'He doesn't know anything,' Hannah said, 'about tests in this area.'

'You didn't go into details, did you?' Val almost hissed her question.

'No, but you were saying you knew who had the commune closed down?'

'I think I know who started all the trouble,' Val said, evading a direct answer.

'Who?'

'Patricia Morris.'

'Mrs Morris?'

'You know what she's like — always poking her nose into what doesn't concern her, and her house does back onto Farmer Tony's field. She was making allegations about the view being spoilt and how she was going to do something about it.'

'She couldn't possibly have seen any of their activities through the trees.'

'According to Jim Matthews she has a powerful pair of binoculars. And she knows how to use them.' The two women exchanged rueful smiles.

'Well I hope she's happy now,' Hannah said. 'She can have her view all to herself.'

'She may wish to have the commune back if our suspicions are correct. She's done us all a disservice. The developers didn't have to go to the bother of having Ronnie and the others moved on. Mrs Morris did their job for them.'

'You mean all that business about contravening a bye-law was unfounded?'

'I don't know the ins and outs but everyone left before any officials turned up to move them on, didn't they?' Val asked.

'Yes.'

'I'm sure they should have been served with official notice to leave. That's the law isn't, it? You have to be given due notice.'

'Now I come to think about it,' Hannah mused, 'Farmer Tony knew nothing about any bye-law.'

'So by moving on everyone played into this scout's hands,' Val concluded.

'We did the job for them.'

'It would seem so.'

'Patricia Morris has a lot to answer for.'

'She did create the opportunity, I'll admit,' Val said. 'I've no evidence that she actually went ahead with her threats to lodge an official complaint, but Jim Matthews overheard her intentions. He's always hanging around listening. He blew the whistle and the whole thing seems to have ballooned.'

'What do you think this scout you mentioned is looking for?' Hannah asked.

'Suitable sites for exploratory drilling for cheap energy? I don't know but there's a lot of land around here, including Farmer Tony's.'

'And you want me to mention this to Ronnie when I see her again?'

'I don't want to stir up more trouble. Perhaps I shouldn't have said anything, only it has been playing on my mind.'

'With my sister's network of contacts it won't be long before she finds out if something's going on, and I think she might have heard something already,' Hannah said as she recalled the original reason why Ronnie wanted her to take up the position of Steve's housekeeper.

'This sort of thing is very unsettling. If you do make enquiries, can you keep my name out of it? I mean, well, Mother relies on me so much. I wouldn't want her upset. We live together and it's a quiet neighbourhood. We'd like to keep it that way.'

Hannah took pity on the older woman. 'Your secret's safe with me, Val. I'm not sure when I'll see Ronnie again, but when I get the chance I'll tell her I heard someone say something and is there any truth in it, something along those lines? Is that suitably vague?'

'That is a weight off my mind, dear. Now tell me about this new stepbrother of yours — Jed, isn't it? Tony's wife Carol was in the library the other day and said he was staying with them for a while, over from America?'

'I haven't heard from him since Ronnie left,' Hannah admitted. 'He said he had some business in London but we plan a get-together when everyone is back.'

'That will be nice.' Val began to gather up her things. 'Now I've taken up quite enough of your time, Hannah. Thank you for the coffee and the little talk. I hope we won't lose touch. You must come and visit me next time. Maybe we could do lunch?'

'I'll look forward to it,' Hannah replied. She watched Val drive away, a thoughtful frown wrinkling her forehead. Jed had told her he was a scout. Was he the one Val had been referring to? If so, she needed to talk to him, and preferably before Ronnie and Xan got wind of things.

'I'm sorry, Hannah,' Carol answered her call. 'Jed's not here.'

'Do you know where I could contact him? Is he in London?'

'I think he's gone back to America.'

'Without telling me?' Hannah gasped. 'It must have been very sudden.'

Carol sounded embarrassed. 'I don't think he was alone.'

'Ronnie hasn't gone with him?' Hannah asked. 'I know they got on very well that night up at the farmhouse, but I thought she was with Xan.'

'Not Ronnie, no. I'm talking about Alison.'

'Alison Cooper?'

'That's right, the one who's engaged to your Mr Talbot. She's gone with him.'

8

'You need to practise driving the four-track.' Steve appeared in the kitchen doorway while Hannah was preparing lunch for herself and Lucy. 'Hello?' He raised his voice when she didn't respond. 'Is anyone at home?'

The tomato she was slicing rolled away from her and landed on the stone floor with an unpleasant splat. The cucumber rolled after it.

'Why don't you throw the lettuce down there as well and make a meal of it?' Steve joked as he bent down to pick them up.

Hannah's head was still reeling from the shock of Carol's news.

'Yuck.' Lucy ran into the kitchen and skidded to a halt as she took in the mess on the floor.

'My thoughts entirely.' Steve looked at her. 'You didn't really fancy salad for lunch, did you?'

Lucy cast a glance at Hannah, then putting a hand to her mouth whispered, 'Ice cream would be brilliant.'

'Great idea. Come on, Hannah — put that knife down before you do any more damage. We are going out for lunch and you are doing the driving.'

'No,' Hannah protested. 'I mean, you've got a busy day. You can't spare the time.'

'Yes I can, and I make the rules. If it makes you feel better I'll take my diving cylinder along with us.'

'Are we going swimming?' Lucy began to look excited.

'Not today, I'm afraid,' Steve apologised. 'It's not warm enough, and I need to exchange my cylinder for a new one. There's a chandler's I go to on the south coast who'll do it for me. They're right by the sea and last time I visited there was a swan nesting. You'd like to see that, Lucy, wouldn't you?'

The child nodded vigorously.

'You mustn't go anywhere near her,'

he warned the child, 'but you can take a look.'

'Shall I go and get my new jumper? The one the ladies at the commune weaved for me?'

'You'd better wash your face too,' Steve added as Hannah still didn't move. 'It's covered in half the garden.'

Lucy ran off to do his bidding.

'Now.' There was no smile on Steve's face as he challenged Hannah. 'What's wrong? Has Miss Lawrence upset you?'

Hannah tried a smile but couldn't really pull it off. 'I telephoned Carol. She's Farmer Tony's wife.'

'And?' Steve prompted.

'I wanted to speak to Jed but he wasn't there.'

'So why do you look paler than a ghost? Here, you'd better sit down.' He thrust her into one of the wooden kitchen chairs. 'What's bugging you?'

'He's gone back to America.'

'Bit of a surprise, I'll admit, but hardly earth-shattering. What was he doing over here anyway? You never did tell me.'

Hannah ignored the question. 'You might as well hear it from me. He wasn't alone.'

Steve finished wiping up the mess from the floor and began rinsing the mop under the tap.

'Right, fine, so now I know. Thank you for updating me on Jed's actions. Are you ready to go out?'

'According to Carol, Alison went with him.'

Water from the cold tap sprayed everywhere as Steve dropped the mop in the sink. He swore loudly, then apologised. 'Sorry. Don't think Lucy heard me.' He turned off the tap. 'Now run that past me again.'

'Alison and Jed are in America.'

'Doing what exactly?'

'I don't know.'

Steve wiped his hands on a tea towel. 'I think I can live with it, and unless you're harbouring any romantic notions about this Jed, I'd say life in Deneham can carry on pretty much as normal, wouldn't you?'

'You don't mind?' Hannah raised her eyes to meet Steve's.

'I told you, Alison and I are not an item. She's a free agent and she can do exactly as she pleases. And if she wants to go to America with Jed, then it's fine by me.'

'I think they met when she left your house keys at the farmhouse.'

'So that's how Jed got hold of them. I did wonder at the time,' Steve admitted.

'Ready.' There was a whirlwind of colour and Lucy raced back into the kitchen wearing jeans and her new bright red jumper.

'Come on, Hannah,' she urged. 'I want to see the nesting swan.'

'Yes, come on, Hannah,' Steve urged her. 'You'd better change your top too. The one you're wearing is covered in tomato pips. I'll get the car out.'

Lucy swung her little satchel excitedly from side to side. 'I'm going to look for some wild flowers to press,' she announced. 'Then I can put them in my book and show Mummy when she gets back.'

'Stir your stumps, Hannah. We can't hang around much longer or the day will be gone. We've got at least an hour's drive ahead of us. We're missing the best part of the day.'

Unable to think of any more excuses not to go on the jaunt with Steve, Hannah went to her room to repair the damage to her blouse and to run a comb through her hair. Her heart was beating uncomfortably fast as she tried to get her head around this latest development.

If Jed had returned to America, then that could mean he had found his site. It had to be farmer Tony's field, but Hannah did not want to go down Patricia Morris's route and start a rumour that might be without foundation.

Neither could she mention her suspicions to Steve. He would immediately think she was accusing him of being involved.

'Aren't you ready yet?' Steve bellowed up the stairs. 'There'll be no ice cream left if you don't get a move on.'

Driving Steve's four-track proved easier than Hannah had feared, and soon they were bowling down the road towards the coast. Hannah's spirits lifted as the sun danced patterns on the dusty bonnet of the serviceable vehicle. The soft Surrey hills gave way to the chalkier Sussex backdrop.

'It says in my book there's orchids and butterflies in Sussex.' Lucy rubbed at a patch of window. 'Do you think we'll see any?'

'How about grasshoppers?' Steve asked. 'Do you like them?'

Lucy squealed. 'They're all green and sticky and they jump in the air.'

'Yup, that's what they do well,' Steve agreed.

Hannah executed a neat gear change as they came to a roundabout.

'You know you can use either of the cars whenever you like?' he said. Steve also drove a conventional saloon car, which Hannah had used to go into town to get supplies. 'Just check that I don't need it first if I'm home. You're covered by my insurance. Forgot to ask, you do have a valid licence with no penalty points?'

Hannah cast him a sideways glance. 'My licence is fine but I haven't driven for over a year. I gave up my car when my hours were cut at the library. It was too expensive to run and I didn't really need it.'

'They say driving is like riding a bike,' Steve replied. 'You never really forget how to do it.'

Seagulls now circled above them, keening in the sea breeze and bringing with them the salty tang of brine.

'That's better,' Steve approved as she smiled. 'For a while back there I thought you were sickening for something. A good dose of sea air will soon put some colour back in your cheeks. Slow down. The turning's along here somewhere.' Hannah eased up on the accelerator. 'Here we are, left now.'

Hannah swung off the coast road, down a bumpy track. 'Are you sure this is right?'

'I know it doesn't look much,' Steve agreed, 'but we're on course. Left again by the hut with all the surfboards outside.'

Hannah followed his instructions. 'Is this where you dive?' From the driving seat, Hannah could see the white crested waves lapping the shore.

'Occasionally. I like to keep my cylinder topped up 'cause I never know when I'm going to need it. Third hut down is what we're looking for.'

'Where's the swan?' Lucy undid her belt with an excited smile.

'Not sure. Why don't you take a walk up there and see what you can find? There are plenty of wild flowers to see as well.' Steve pointed in the direction of some more huts. 'She'll be fine,' he added to Hannah. 'Old Joe who mends nets will keep an eye on her.'

'Do you need any help?' Hannah asked as Steve lugged the cylinder out of the back of the car.

'Think I can manage, thanks.' He manhandled it onto the shingle, then rolled it across to the chandler's. 'Mind your head.' He ducked to avoid a low beam. 'And careful you don't trip. There are ropes and all sorts of hazards to be wary of.'

The inside of the hut smelt of sisal and damp rubber.

'G'day,' a blond bronzed surfer type greeted them with a friendly smile. 'Want an exchange?'

'Please.'

'The forecast isn't too brilliant,' he said as he swapped the cylinders over, 'if you're thinking of going out.'

'Not today,' Steve replied.

'Family, is it?' He turned his blue eyes in Hannah's direction. 'Nice day for a picnic with your wife. Have a good one.'

'Thanks, we will,' Steve replied.

'No worries, just watch out for the storm that's brewing.'

'Why didn't you explain?' Hannah

demanded back at the car.

'Explain what?' Steve looked puzzled.

'That we're not husband and wife?'

'Did you want me to also tell him that Lucy isn't our daughter and risk getting arrested for abducting a minor?'

'Of course not. You know what I mean. Never mind.' Hannah gave up and shading her eyes against the bright sunshine asked, 'Where is Lucy?'

'Let's go find her.'

They heard the child's excited chatter before they rounded the corner. A weather-beaten fisherman with a white beard and puffing on a pipe was attending to his nets while Lucy explained the reason for their visit.

'We're going to have ice cream,' she announced.

'At Katie's hut, eh? She's got the best vanilla I've ever tasted and I've travelled far and wide.'

'Does she do sprinkles?' Lucy asked, an earnest look on her face.

'I expect she'll find you a bit of chocolate if that's what takes your fancy. There now, here's your folks come to fetch you. All done?'

Lucy leapt out of the rowing boat she had been sitting in while she chatted to Joe and ran towards them.

'Don't forget your jumper,' Hannah called out.

'It's too hot,' Lucy complained as she went back for it.

'Then tie it around your waist. I don't want you losing it.'

Grumbling, Lucy did as she was told. 'The swan isn't nesting this year. Joe says it's too noisy here and she might be further up the beach and he knows all about wild flowers and fish. In the summer he goes out every day and he gets lobsters and prawns and crab. Can we go to Katie's hut now for our ice cream?' Lucy tugged at Hannah's hand and dragged her across the shingle. 'Come and see the rock pool. I found a crab,' she announced. 'It was tiny so I threw it back. What's that funny green stuff?'

'Rock samphire.' Steve joined them. 'You can eat it.'

Lucy pulled a face. ''spect Mummy would like it.'

'Right, who's for ice cream?' Steve asked.

'Me!' Lucy danced on the shingle.

'This way.'

They struggled up the beach. Hannah was glad she'd worn the sensible shoes she used to visit the commune. It was difficult to keep up with Steve's long strides and more than once she lost her footing. Lucy giggled as they both slid backwards.

'Come on, slowcoaches,' Steve called out from higher up the beach. 'Last one at Katie's buys the ices.'

Lucy began to run and easily overtook Steve, who held out a hand to help Hannah out of her predicament.

'I won, I won!' Lucy crowed.

'Looks like it's my wrap,' Steve said.

'You don't have to,' Hannah insisted. 'I've got some money and it really ought to be our treat.'

'My suggestion. I'm paying,' he insisted.

They reached the pretty striped beach hut, displaying an impressive range of beach paraphernalia from buckets and spades to little flags for sandcastles, windmills that whirred in the breeze, sun hats and lotions.

'Hello, my darlings.' A red-faced woman emerged from the back. 'Is it my vanilla you're after? Got a text from Joe. He said you were on your way up.'

'I didn't know he was into technology.' Steve ordered a double cone for Lucy.

'He's out in all weathers. His wife insisted he get a mobile phone after a nasty incident couple of years back.' She added an extra scoop for Lucy. 'There you are, my lovely. Careful you don't drop it. Same for you, is it?' she looked at Hannah. 'You need feeding up, my girl. Sit down at one of my little tables and I'll bring them over.'

'There you go.' Steve drew out a chair for Hannah. 'Make yourself comfortable. I know there are slats missing.' He lowered his voice. 'But we won't mention it. Wouldn't want to hurt Katie's feelings for the world.'

'How long have you known her?'

'Forever,' Steve replied. 'She's part of the scenery. Joe's her brother-in-law.'

Katie served up their ice cream. 'Thought you'd prefer yours in a dish,' she said to Steve and Hannah.

'Thanks, Katie. You're a star.'

'Where's the little maid?' she asked.

'Gone to inspect the rock pool.'

'I'd keep an eye on the weather if I were you. See those clouds on the horizon? They're trouble.'

By the time Hannah has scooped up the last mouthful of the most delicious ice cream she had ever eaten, the sky was turning grey and Katie's awning was flapping in the wind.

'Better take the buckets in,' she said. 'Don't want them bowling up the beach.' As she spoke a violent gust of wind blew her sign over.

'We'd better get a move on,' Steve said. 'Where's Lucy?'

Hannah scanned the beach. A fat

blob of rain landed on her arm.

'Lucy,' she cupped her hands and called out, 'come on.'

More rain began to fall and within moments the shingle was glistening wet.

'She can't have gone far.' Hannah's blouse was now wringing wet and her hair plastered to her forehead.

'I think she went this way.' Steve dragged Hannah down the slippery slope to the beach. Something bright red that had been tied to the breakwater flapped at them.

'That's her jumper!' Hannah shrieked and snatched it up. It was a sodden mass. The rain was now torrential. Hannah could hardly breathe as she looked around the deserted beach.

'Lucy,' Steve bellowed, 'where are you?' His breath misted the air.

There was no reply.

9

Heads turned to look at the source of the roar of the motorbike engine revving up at the traffic lights. Patricia Morris pursed her lips as Xan waved in her direction.

'See, you couldn't keep 'em down, Patti.' Jim Matthews jostled her at the pedestrian crossing before adding, 'In case you hadn't noticed, they're back.'

'I can see that for myself, thank you.'

'Wonder where they're going to set up home next?'

'I have no idea.'

The crossing light changed from red to green and Patricia took brisk steps forward, hoping to lose Jim Matthews. It didn't work.

'Seems you jumped the gun a bit there, didn't you?' Jim tagged along beside her.

'I don't know what you mean.'

'There were no plans to evict the commune.'

'I didn't say there were.'

'Didn't you?' Jim raised his eyebrows. 'I must have got the wrong end of the stick.'

The increased throttle from the motorbike made further conversation impossible as Xan eased slowly forward. Seizing her opportunity, Patricia scuttled away from Jim. All that had happened at Tony's farm had played on her conscience. Things had happened swiftly after she enquired about registering her complaint and by the time she came downstairs for breakfast the following morning the field was deserted.

The sound of motorbikes revving up had drawn her attention to the window, and taking up her binoculars she saw to her consternation that the settlement was no longer there and cows were beginning to amble back into the field. She couldn't help feeling what she had done was a mean trick, even if she hadn't been directly responsible for the commune closure.

Having the commune in the next field had in some ways enriched her days and given her purpose. Now they stretched aimlessly in front of her. Word had got round that she had had a hand in what had happened and local opinion, while not openly hostile, was frosty. It had done no good trying to explain her side of things. People were not in the mood to listen. It seemed the commune had more support than Patricia realised. Her offer of volunteer support at the community centre providing some temporary housing help was politely but firmly turned down. The rebuff hurt. Patricia cared for the welfare of Deneham and she sensed had her husband still been alive he would have been disappointed in her.

Harlequin tugged at his lead. 'Stop that,' Patricia snapped at the dog. Not looking where she was going, the lead became entangled around her shopping bag and in the ensuing confusion she bumped into another pedestrian. With Harlequin barking excitedly at her heels, Patricia did her best to extricate her shopping from the lead.

'If it isn't Mrs Morris.' There was laughter in the voice that greeted her. 'I'd recognise those sensible shoes anywhere. Here, let me help.'

'Who? I mean what?' She blinked as the buxom woman who was bending down took charge of the situation.

'Soon have you straightened out,' she beamed up at the disconcerted older woman.

'I'm sorry, I don't recall,' she began. 'Have we met?'

'Babs Beckett. Lavender, that is. Surely you haven't forgotten me — the bane of your well-ordered life? Ronnie and Hannah's mother?'

Patricia gasped. 'You look different.' The words were out before Patricia realised how impolite they sounded, but there was no denying Babs Beckett had changed, and for the better. She was now a sun-kissed statuesque mid-blonde beauty. The last time Patricia Morris had seen her, she had been chained to a bench in the park, demonstrating against the proposed closure of the recreation area. She seemed to remember Babs had chalked up a victory on that one.

'Come and have a coffee and we'll catch up,' Babs suggested. 'That's if you're not too busy?'

Curiosity got the better of Patricia's scruples and she meekly followed Babs into the coffee shop.

'Do you do cappuccino, Mrs Morris?' Babs asked.

'I'd prefer tea.'

'Of course you would.'

Patricia flushed. Babs always sounded as though she were teasing, yet underneath the banter it was as if she understood the older woman.

'I think after all this time you could call me Patricia,' she said in a gruff voice.

The dimple in Babs's cheek deepened. 'Patricia it is then.' She located the best window seats and after giving their order to the hovering waitress, settled down opposite her ex-neighbour.

'So you're remarried?' It was Patricia who asked the first question.

'That's right.'

'Where's this new husband of yours?'

'In Texas.'

'He didn't come with you?'

'He's got a lot of work to catch up on after our honeymoon cruise in the Caribbean.'

'Is it true he's a cowboy?'

'Glad to see the old homestead is keeping up its standards gossip-wise.' Babs looked amused at the description of her husband. 'Hal's more than a cowboy. He owns a huge ranch. It's a thriving business and he employs several staff. I hope to help him run things but I had to come back to see my girls. I left in such a hurry I didn't have time to say a proper goodbye.'

'Steve Talbot wasn't best pleased.' Patricia was unable to keep a note of satisfaction out of her voice as she imparted her nugget of information. 'He shouted at poor little Hannah.'

'I've brought both my daughters up

to take care of themselves, Patricia, so I'm sure Hannah gave as good as she got.'

'She did actually,' Patricia admitted with a reluctant smile. 'She's spunky, I'll give her that, and in quite a different way from your Ronnie.'

'Hannah's quiet,' Babs agreed, 'but she knows her own mind.'

Their refreshments arrived and Patricia busied herself pouring out her tea, while Babs scooped up the froth from her cappuccino and licked it off her spoon with relish.

'I bumped into one the nurses who help run the crèche at the community centre. I understand you had a hand in moving Ronnie on?' Babs said.

A guilty flush stained the base of Patricia's neck. 'I might have expressed an objection to the commune's presence, but I wasn't instrumental in the outcome.'

Babs continued licking her spoon like a cat enjoying a saucer of cream. 'Don't worry,' she soothed, 'I understand. You

130

didn't like the commune. They've gone. Problem solved.'

Patricia blinked. She had never been sure what to make of Babs. The two women had frequently crossed swords, but she couldn't help being fascinated by the woman seated opposite her. She reminded Patricia of a butterfly in her multi-coloured kaftan. The colours fluttered as she moved her hands when she spoke. It was easy to be dazzled by Babs Beckett.

'Did you see your son-in-law just now?' Patricia changed the subject.

'On that huge great bike by the lights?' Babs nodded. 'He drove off before I could speak to him. Harlequin wasn't totally responsible for us bumping into each other. I was trying to see where Xan was headed. I thought Ronnie might be with him, but she wasn't riding pillion. You don't know where she's gone? The nurse couldn't tell me.'

Patricia shook her head, feeling another twinge of guilt. 'Did you know

Hannah's taken over your job as housekeeper to Steve Talbot?' she said, 'and that Lucy's gone with her?'

'I've been up to the house but it's deserted. No one's in. I rang the bell several times and walked round the back. They must have gone out for the day.'

'When you went off so suddenly . . . ' Patricia chose her words carefully.

'Yes?' Babs encouraged after she lapsed into silence.

'Mr Talbot wasn't best pleased.'

'He had no reason to be dissatisfied. Hannah got the job of housekeeper and I got the new husband.'

'That's rather a flippant way of looking at things,' Patricia chided Babs.

'How would you have me look at them?' she asked.

'I'm not sure really,' was the flustered reply.

'You know, I expect Xan was on his way to his mother's,' Babs said.

'That gypsy who lives in the forest?' Patricia's prejudices resurfaced. Biting her tongue, she only just managed to stop herself saying she should be moved on too.

'She isn't actually a gypsy, she just embraces the lifestyle and she doesn't do any harm,' Babs insisted. 'Actually I think I'll go and visit her myself. If Xan's there he can update me on all that's been going on.' Babs rose to her feet. 'My treat,' she said, placing a note on the table. 'Keep the change,' she said to the waitress.

'You haven't finished your coffee,' Patricia protested.

'You have the rest if you fancy it. I'm afraid I've nabbed all the froth.'

All eyes watched the beautiful woman in the butterfly dress as she drifted out of the coffee shop and, still with a smile on her face, made her way up the high street.

'Well, really,' Patricia muttered, biting into one of the biscuits Babs had left on the plate. She never had and never would understand any of that family.

Etaine greeted her son as he parked his bike under the trees and strode towards her. 'It's been a time since you visited,' she chided him. She was sitting outside her brightly coloured caravan, shelling peas into a colander.

'I've been a bit busy, Ma.' Her son kissed her cheek.

'Where's the little one?'

'Lucy's with Hannah.'

'Best place for her.' Etaine nodded. 'Want some cider?'

'Please.'

'There's a fresh jug inside. Help yourself.'

Xan sat on the steps beside his mother.

'What's been happening?' she asked.

'Ronnie and I took off to see if we could find a new place to live.'

'And have you?'

'Not sure. She's with some friends at the moment but she wants to move back soon as she can. Farmer Tony may re-let the field to the commune if they can get this bye-law thing sorted out.'

'Ronnie ought to do something, if only for Lucy's sake. A daughter needs to be with her mother. It's time your Ronnie settled down and stopped gallivanting about the countryside.'

Etaine carried on shelling her peas. Xan sipped his cider. The air was cool and fresh in the forest. Sunlight dappled the trees. Squirrels darted in and out the foliage and rabbits rummaged in the undergrowth. The air smelt of damp earth and vaporised motorbike fuel. A flash of bright colour caught the corner of Xan's eye.

'Babs?' he stood up. 'I thought you were in America.'

'It really is me,' she laughed. 'Hello, Etaine. Good to see you.' The two women kissed.

'Mind if I join you?'

'You'll spoil that lovely dress if you sit there.'

'A bit of dirt never worried me,' Babs replied. 'You get covered in all sorts of things when you're protesting.'

'I thought you'd gone over to the other side, marrying a rich Texan,' Xan said.

'Hal may own a ranch, but he's as much into green issues as I am.'

'What's he like, this Texan of yours?'

'We met online,' Babs laughed. 'It's the modern way of doing things, but I never thought anything like this would happen to me. I was trawling this site for singles and his face popped up. I liked his looks, we exchanged a few emails, and the next thing I knew he was proposing to me.'

'And you accepted?' Etaine said.

'Chances like that don't come twice. You bet I did,' Babs replied, 'and we couldn't be happier. He's kind and thoughtful and a real gentleman.'

'His son was over here last week,' Xan said.

'Jed?' The smile left Babs's face.

'Don't you like your new stepson?' Etaine was quick to pick up on Babs's disquiet.

'There are a few people in this world I don't trust,' Babs replied.

'He's one of them?' Xan asked.

'He wasn't too happy about Hal and me getting married. I can understand that, but when we were alone he made unpleasant insinuations about my past. I know I've led a colourful life, but I've never gone against the law.'

'You've sailed close to it once or twice,' Etaine interrupted.

'I got the feeling Jed's feelings went deeper than jealousy. He's back in the States now. He came to visit us and he brought Alison Cooper with him. I recognised her from my days working for Steve Talbot. It was then I realised he had been over here and introduced himself to Ronnie and Hannah. My maternal instinct kicked in. Something wasn't right and I knew I had to fly over and check things out.'

Etaine nodded agreement. 'You were right to come.'

'I didn't tell anyone of my plans, so no one was here to meet me. The only person I could find was you, Xan, and I bumped into Mrs Morris, who says I can now call her Patricia.'

'She's not so bad,' Etaine said. 'I know she wants me evicted too, but she's only exercising her rights.'

'That's very generous of you,' Babs said.

Etaine shrugged. 'I understand.'

'I think you overreacted to the situation, Babs.' Xan finished his cider. 'Jed's bound to be a bit bugged because his father's married again, but things'll settle down. You'll see.'

'I hope so.' Babs didn't look convinced.

'Want me to give you a lift anywhere?' Xan nodded towards his bike. 'I've a spare helmet and the fresh air might help to clear your head.'

'It's been a while since I've felt the wind in my hair.' Babs leapt to her feet. 'Full throttle?'

'Careful now,' Etaine warned them. 'Neither of you are as young as you used to be.'

'Ma, I'm only thirty-five,' Xan protested.

'You're talking to your mother, remember.' Etaine looked squarely at her son. 'I know exactly how many years ago I gave birth to you.'

'And we all know you're closer to forty than thirty,' Babs laughed, 'but I'm not counting. Come on, Tiger. Let's hit the open road.'

10

The rain stung Hannah's face as it fell relentlessly from the leaden sky.

'Lucy,' her voice was a tortured wail. 'Where are you?'

Her breath came in heaving sobs as she flicked wet hair out of her eyes. The waves crashed against the beach, huge grey-crested monsters. Hannah licked sea salt from her lips. This was a nightmare of the worst kind. Angry clouds scudded across the horizon. A swirling mist rising off the sea now obliterated the breakwater. Hannah twisted Lucy's jumper in her hands.

'Hannah . . . ' A thin voice floated across the mist.

'Lucy,' she shrieked, 'is that you?' Hannah held her breath. Was the wind playing tricks? Stumbling forward, no longer able to make out where she was going, Hannah tripped over some driftwood. As she went sprawling she saw Lucy, her leg buckled underneath her body at an unnatural angle, her face twisted in pain.

The child gave a small moan. Hannah scrambled towards her but Steve raced past.

'Let me do this,' he ordered. 'I've had plenty of experience with falls.'

'Don't hurt her.' Hannah wanted to pick up the child herself, but Steve was stronger, and she could tell from the trust in Lucy's eyes that the child felt safe with him.

'Can you move at all, Lucy?' Steve asked gently.

'A little bit.' Lucy bit her lip. 'I was running after a dog and I tripped. He was brown and white and his fur was getting wet.'

'You can tell us all about it later. Right now we have to get you home. Can you put your arms round my neck?'

'Yes.' Lucy did as she was told.

'That's the ticket.' Steve smiled at her.

'You're very wet,' Lucy complained.

'So are you,' he retaliated.

'Why did you take your jumper off?' Hannah demanded, still clutching the sodden garment as Steve began to move.

'Got hot,' Lucy said, her eyelids drooping.

Despite his burden, Steve's long strides soon ate up the distance to the car.

'You found her then? Poor little mite.' Katie bustled over from her kiosk. 'Here's a towel and some dry blankets and a thermos. She needs something warm inside her. Let me help you.'

Leaving the two women to dry the child in the back of their vehicle and make sure she was comfortable, Steve tousled his wet hair with a spare towel. Then, scrambling into the front seat, he turned the ignition and set the heater to full blast. 'There, that should do the trick.'

Katie tucked Lucy into the last of the blankets. 'You can bring them back next time you visit,' she said to Hannah. 'Now off you go.'

'I'll drive,' Steve said. 'You stay in the back and keep an eye on Lucy.'

The child's head had fallen forward and her eyes were closed. Hannah put a hand to her forehead.

'Her face is flushed but that might be from the hot tea.'

'Has her ankle swelled up?'

Hannah gently removed Lucy shoes. She didn't stir in her sleep. 'I don't think so.'

'That's a blessing.'

'Do you think she'll be all right?'

'She couldn't have been there long. If she hasn't caught cold in the rain she'll be fine.'

Hannah shivered.

'Are you OK?' Steve glanced at the rear-view mirror.

'I'm warm and dry now. Katie saw to that.' Hannah smiled.

'She's a good sort.' The engine purred as they reached the main road and Steve put his foot down on the accelerator. 'If we don't meet too much traffic, hopefully we'll be home within the hour.'

'I can't believe how quickly the storm came down.' Hannah shivered again at the memory of the rain pounding the seafront.

'One of the first lessons I learned when I was diving. Never underestimate nature. It can be your friend one minute and your enemy the next. Would you look at that?' He gestured out of the window as he drove along. The grey skies had miraculously cleared and the sun now shone down from a brilliant blue sky. 'Proves my point, wouldn't you say? The roads here are completely dry. They haven't had a drop of rain.' He turned down the heater control. Lucy stirred, then closed her eyes again.

'I'm sorry we had such a sad end to our day out,' Hannah apologised.

'It could have been a lot worse.'

'This wasn't what you bargained for, was it?'

'What wasn't?' He frowned at Hannah.

'Playing nursemaid to your house-keeper and her niece.'

'It's never happened to me before, I'll

admit, but I've had to act as a nursemaid several times in some of the places I've visited.'

'What sorts of things have you had to deal with?' Hannah asked, intrigued.

'Insect bites, snakes, food poisoning, falls, blood issues . . . You name it, I've dealt with it. On one tour I was appointed unofficial medical officer. That wasn't a trip I enjoyed, but I learned a lot.'

'Didn't you have a doctor with you?'

'We did, but he was allergic to nuts, a minor detail he didn't mention before we set out. We were based in South America, so it wasn't long before he came out in a rash. He was a very junior doctor and he thought if he didn't eat any nuts he wouldn't be affected.' Steve raised his eyes in exasperation. 'Things got worse. He was sent home in an air ambulance and it was left to yours truly to carry the medical bag.'

'You could have come home too,' Hannah said.

'We could have done, but everything

was set up. It would have meant losing a lot of money, not to mention time and location. Everyone else was up for it, so we went on. It's not a trip I remember with any affection. A twisted ankle and a bit of rain on a beach in the south of England is minor stuff in comparison.'

As they sped along Hannah began to relax. For a committed bachelor, Steve had displayed a remarkable ability not to flap in a family crisis.

'Sometimes it would be useful to be able to contact Ronnie by mobile phone,' Hannah said, 'but she's always been hopeless with technology, ever since school.'

'I always wanted to be out and about doing things too.' Steve changed gear. 'I only learned to use a computer because I had to.' He pulled off the main road. 'Not far now.'

'I'll give Lucy a warm bath and put her to bed as soon as we get back, if that's all right with you.'

'I'm a dab hand at baked beans if you fancy some for supper.'

'I should be doing the cooking. It's what I'm paid for.'

'Don't turn down the offer. It's the only thing I know how to make, although I could if stretched manage cheese on toast.' They drew into the forecourt of Highworth House. 'You see to Lucy while I garage the car. There's plenty of hot water, so get yourself a bath too.'

'What about you?'

'I've a bit of work to see to, so why don't we have our bean feast at — ' He glanced at his watch. ' — seven o'clock in the kitchen?'

Lucy was almost asleep by the time Hannah had bathed her, made a hot water bottle and put her to bed. She waited until Lucy was breathing deeply before leaving the room. She ran more water for her own bath and, sinking into the scented bubbles, wallowed in a haze of lavender steam.

Until Lucy's mishap she had enjoyed the day. Steve had proved an entertaining companion. She tried to convince herself it was the warmth of the bath bringing a flush to her cheeks and not an increase in temperature caused from thinking about Steve Talbot. He was hardly likely to be interested in someone like Hannah. He was a man of the world who had visited far-flung countries Hannah had only ever read about in travel brochures and books from the library. Her life had been Deneham and coping with her volatile family. As individuals she and Steve couldn't be more different, yet there was something about him that set her pulses racing.

She forced herself to think about other things. She wondered where her mother was and when she would be in touch again. Hannah squeezed hot water out of her sponge and dribbled it down her face.

There was no way Hannah could afford the fare to Texas, and although she knew Hal was the sort of man to pay for her to visit, there was something about the gesture that didn't sit quite right with Hannah.

Then there was his son Jed. She thought she had liked him, but was he this scout everyone was talking about? And what of Alison? If the gossip was correct, she was in America with Jed. It was all too much for Hannah to take in and she was certain there was more disruption to come.

Easing out of the old-fashioned stand-alone bath, Hannah grabbed one of the fluffy towels she had found in the linen cupboard and wrapped it round her body. She washed her hair, too, and as she rubbed it dry she imagined what it would be like to feel Steve's hands in her hair. Drying your partner's hair, she thought, must be one of the nicest things to do.

Catching a glimpse of her reflection in the steamed-up bathroom mirror, she caught her breath. It had to be the condensation making her eyes look bright and the heat from the bath causing her complexion to be so rosy. No other explanation was possible, she told herself firmly as she finished towelling her hair.

Time was getting on and she had better things to do than moon about the place looking at her reflection in the mirror. Shrugging on a shower robe, she belted it firmly about her waist before going back in the bedroom to check on Lucy.

The child's face was as flushed as Hannah's. Hannah put a hand on Lucy's forehead. It felt warm but Hannah didn't think she was running a temperature. Tucking the bedclothes around Lucy's sleeping form, Hannah went to her own room and put on a clean blouse and a fresh skirt. All their clothes they had worn earlier were still sodden and in a pile on the floor where Hannah had tossed them in her hurry to attend to Lucy. Picking them up, she inhaled the evocative smell of the sea. It brought a smile of memory to her face.

There was just time to put the dirty laundry in the washing machine before her seven o'clock date with Steve in the kitchen. As she emerged from the utility room, the aroma of burnt toast wafted through from the kitchen, followed by some colourful invective.

'Yet again I'm glad Lucy isn't around to hear you.' Hannah stood in the doorway and watched Steve deal ineffectively with a toaster stubbornly refusing to release its contents.

'The blasted thing's stuck.' He coughed then raised pleading eyes in her direction. 'What do I do?'

'Turn it off at the wall to start with,' Hannah instructed, throwing open the windows to clear the atmosphere.

There was a click as Steve snapped off the power supply.

'Then what?' he asked.

'Then,' Hannah smiled sweetly, 'you start again.'

'Can you do it?' Steve asked with a pleading look on his face. 'I'll admit I was showing off when I said I could do toast.'

The pan of beans bubbling on the cooker chose that moment to boil over.

With a yell of panic, Steve grabbed up the saucepan, then threw it with the contents into the sink.

'The handle's hot,' he gasped, his eyes watering.

'What did you expect?' Hannah, too, now began coughing as the smell of burnt beans mingled with that of the toast.

Steve rubbed a hand through his hair. 'Kitchen looks like a war zone, doesn't it?' he said.

Hannah hid her smile with difficulty. Steve had daubed a trail of burnt breadcrumbs on his forehead. It made him look like an ancient warrior coated in war paint and ready for action.

'It's not that funny,' he complained.

'Have you tried looking in the mirror?' Hannah lost her battle with her self-control and burst into laughter.

'Good grief.' Steve began rubbing vigorously at his forehead. 'I've only ever done soup on a camping gas stove before,' he admitted. 'I thought it couldn't be that difficult to do toast and heat up some beans.'

'It isn't,' Hannah sympathised, 'but I don't think you're a natural.'

'I've got some bad news,' Steve confessed.

'What?' Hannah asked with a pang of concern.

'That was our last tin of beans, and the bread's run out.' He paused. 'There's no need to wail about it,' he said.

'I wasn't.' The cry galvanised Hannah into action. 'That was Lucy.'

11

For the second time that day, Hannah nursed Lucy in the back seat of the four-track as Steve broke every record getting to the hospital.

'We don't want to be stopped by the police,' Hannah called out from the back seat as they swerved around yet another corner, almost clipping the kerb.

'Yes we do,' Steve insisted. 'We need an escort.'

'Red light!' Hannah shrieked as Steve screeched to a halt.

'How is she?' He cast an anxious look over his shoulder.

'Burning up,' Hannah said as she felt Lucy's face.

They had both raced upstairs when she had called out in distress, to find Lucy had thrown off all the bedclothes and was thrashing around the sheets.

What she was saying didn't make any sense.

'Do you know what to do?' Steve's muscles were firm under her fingers as Hannah grasped his arm.

'My medical skills don't go that far. We've got to get her to accident and emergency. Can you carry her downstairs while I go for the car?'

Wrapping Lucy in one of Katie's discarded blankets, Hannah carefully carried her burden down the stairs. The night was warm but Hannah's teeth were chattering with fear. Her head was full of 'if only's. If only Lucy hadn't taken off her jumper she wouldn't have caught cold, and if only she hadn't raced after that dog she wouldn't have tripped, and none of this would have happened if only they'd stayed at home for the day.

It was difficult holding Lucy still. Hannah had struggled to do up the fretful child's seat belt. Eventually it had clicked into place, but not before her eye had come into contact with

Lucy's flailing fist. The socket throbbed and Hannah suspected she was going to have a black eye in the morning, but right now that was the least of her concerns.

She wished she could contact Ronnie or her mother, but there was no one else she could turn to but Steve, who was now driving like a man possessed through the evening streets. Behind them they heard the wail of a siren.

'At last, the police.' Steve pulled over. 'Leave the explaining to me,' he said.

It wasn't the police, it was an ambulance; and as it sailed past them, Steve gunned their engine into life and took off behind it.

'What are you doing?' Hannah demanded.

'Following it to the hospital. Hold tight. Soon be there.'

'Mummy,' Lucy moaned.

'Hush.' Hannah cradled her. 'We'll see Mummy soon. Right now we have to get you better.'

The silence that greeted her words

was more terrifying than the child's earlier moaning.

'What's happened?' Steve glanced in the mirror.

'I'm not sure. Step on it,' she begged.

'I'm going as fast as I can. I hope this wretched ambulance is going to our hospital and not on its way to London.'

A sob caught in Hannah's throat. This was all her fault.

Lights arced through the encroaching night sky as the Victorian building loomed into view. They followed the ambulance around the roundabout and into the complex. As they came to a halt by accident and emergency, Steve was out of his driver's seat and racing through the sliding glass doors while Hannah was still struggling to undo Lucy's seat belt.

She felt a cold draught of air as the door was wrenched open and a man in a white coat smiled at her. 'No need to worry,' he soothed, 'you're here now. Is this the little lady?'

'Careful.' Hannah managed to keep

her voice steady but inside she wanted to scream at the man.

He smiled reassuringly. 'I won't drop her,' he said. 'Why don't you join your husband at the desk and give all the details to the nurse on duty?'

Steve was pacing up and down by the doors. 'There you are.' He pulled Hannah aside as another orderly appeared with a trolley and Lucy was gently laid on it.

'Where are you taking her?'

'To be examined. Don't worry. She'll be fine.'

'You don't understand,' Hannah began.

'If I could take a few details?' the nurse intervened in a calm voice. 'The sooner we have them the sooner we can find out what's wrong. Now, name and age?'

'I'm twenty-four and my name's Hannah.'

'I meant the little girl.' The nurse did her best to conceal an impatient sigh.

'Sorry.' Hannah put a hand to her throbbing eye. 'Lucy's six.'

'Are you her next of kin?'

'Her mother is her next of kin.'

'Where is her mother now?'

'I don't know.'

The nurse frowned. 'And you are?'

'I'm her mother's sister.'

'Is this gentleman her father?' She looked at Steve.

'No.'

'Anyone own a black four-track? It's blocking an emergency vehicle,' a security guard bellowed.

'I'm going to have to leave you to deal with this on your own.' Steve acknowledged the guard. 'Coming.'

'If you wouldn't mind getting a move on, sir.'

'I'll be back as soon as I can,' Steve promised.

'Are you sure you have no idea of the whereabouts of Lucy's parents?' the nurse demanded.

Hannah found it difficult to think straight and she could feel her control of the situation slipping away. 'I'll try to get hold of them,' Hannah promised out of nowhere. It was a fib but she had to say something to get through to the nurse.

'Have you been the victim of domestic abuse?' the nurse asked.

'What?'

'Your eye is badly bruised.'

'That was Lucy. She lashed out in the car.'

'If you'd like to take a seat,' the nurse said, indicating some orange plastic chairs, 'you'll be called as soon as we have anything to report.'

Hannah sat down, welcoming the hardness of the seat. Why had the nurse sounded as though she didn't believe her?

A sea of anxious faces surrounded Hannah, their eyes fixed hopefully on the connecting doors leading to the examination areas. Hannah glanced at her watch. It was only a quarter to eight — less than three quarters of an hour since Steve had burnt the toast. How could so much have happened in such a short space of time?

And where was Steve? It couldn't

take that long to park a car. Had he deserted her too? She had never felt so lonely in her life. There was no one she could contact. Her mother was in America and goodness knew where Xan and Ronnie were. Scared she was going to be sick, Hannah closed her eyes.

'I've brought you some coffee.' Steve sniffed the steaming liquid in the plastic cup. 'At least I think that's what it is. Hey, steady, it's hot.'

Coffee dribbled over the plastic seat from where Hannah had grabbed his hand.

'Where've you been?'

'It took an age to find a parking space, then I realised I didn't have any change for the meter. If it hadn't been for an elderly couple helping me out I'd be there now. Now drink up.'

The coffee was warm and went some way towards reviving Hannah's jaded spirits.

'That's better. Now update me.' Steve threw the two plastic cups into the waste bin.

'They've taken Lucy away. I don't know where she's gone or what's happening to her, and they won't tell me anything because I'm not her next of kin.'

'Steady,' Steve said in a reassuring voice.

'They think I'm the victim of domestic abuse. They probably think I've poisoned Lucy.'

'Now hold on.' Steve grabbed her hands. 'Tell me exactly what has been happening.'

'My black eye — they think you gave it to me and that we've been mistreating Lucy.'

'That's ridiculous.'

'I tried to tell the nurse it was an accident but she didn't believe me.'

'I suppose they have to be sure,' Steve said, examining Hannah's eye, 'and it is swollen.'

'I want to see Lucy.' Hannah wriggled away from him. Steve put out a hand to detain her. 'Let go of me!' she shrieked.

The security guard approached. 'Is

this gentleman bothering you, madam?'

'He won't let me see Lucy.'

Steve raised his eyes in exasperation. 'I was only trying to explain there's nothing to worry about.'

The security guard ignored Steve. 'And who is Lucy?' he asked Hannah.

'My niece,' she replied.

'We brought her in,' Steve began to explain, 'because she was running a fever.'

'Would you like to sit somewhere else?' the guard asked Hannah. 'I could get someone to attend to your eye.' His glance fell to where Hannah was rubbing her wrist from where Steve had tried to restrain her. 'You'll be quite safe,' the guard added.

'She's safe now, thank you,' Steve clipped back.

'I'm sure the lady can answer for herself.'

'Yes,' Hannah nodded, 'sorry. This gentleman is my employer. He gave us a lift to the hospital.'

'If there's any more trouble, you

know where to find me.' The guard moved away, but not before he cast a warning look in Steve's direction.

'Why does no one believe anything we say?' Hannah hissed at Steve.

'It's probably because we're creating a bit of a commotion. I'm sure Lucy's got nothing more than a chill, and by tomorrow we'll be wondering what all the fuss was about.'

'Where've they taken her?'

From time to time names were called out and the waiting patients were led into the cubicles.

'We've been here over an hour.' Hannah glanced at the clock. 'It can't have taken that long to attend to her. She'll be frightened if she wakes up and doesn't know where she is and is surrounded by a room full of strangers.'

'I'll ask at the desk.' Steve stood up. 'By the way, what is Lucy's name?'

'Sorry?' Hannah blinked at him in confusion.

'Is it Lavender, or did she take her father's surname? It's no wonder that nurse is giving us odd looks when I don't even know the full name of the child I was bringing in.'

'Ronnie kept her maiden name. It's Lucy Lavender.'

Steve strode to the desk. 'We've been waiting for over an hour,' he began.

'We are very busy, sir. You haven't been forgotten,' the nurse reassured him.

'What are they doing?' he demanded. 'The name's Lucy Lavender. She's six years old.'

'They'll attend to the little girl as soon as possible.'

The telephone rang constantly and realising he was keeping the duty nurse from answering another emergency, Steve went back to his seat.

'It's all in hand,' he replied to Hannah's anxious look of enquiry. 'Would you like anything to eat?' he asked.

She shook her head. 'I couldn't.'

'Mrs Lavender?' Hannah leapt to her feet as a white-coated member of the medical staff called out her name.

'Yes?'

'Would you like to come through?'

* * *

'It's very dark,' Babs complained as she and Xan stood by the front door of Highworth House. 'Ring the bell again.'

It echoed throughout the house. 'Sounds like no one's in,' Xan said.

'Where can they be?' Babs looked around. 'If only I'd hung onto my house keys, we could have snuck in. There's a convenient window by the kitchen door. We could try getting in that way.'

'I hope you're not suggesting a spot of housebreaking?' Xan rebuked his mother-in-law. 'My standing with the local constabulary is not very high. I dread to think what would happen if I was caught on the premises without the owner's permission.'

Babs made a gesture of irritation. 'Then what do you suggest we do?'

'Want me to take a look at this convenient kitchen window?'

'Good idea.'

'You stay there in case someone answers the door.'

Babs had never noticed how eerie the garden looked in the twilight. She had always been too busy with her chores to take time for a stroll outside. Now she wished she had. She wasn't of a nervous disposition, but she couldn't identify several of the menacing shapes looming at her out of the half-light. She hoped that whatever was making scuffling noises in the undergrowth would decide to take off to a new venue. Why hadn't she thought to bring a torch?

A loud crashing through the hydrangea bush signalled Xan's return. 'Sorry,' he apologised, 'got caught up in the darkness.'

'What did you find out?'

'Not much. The garage door is open and I spotted some of Ronnie's banners inside.'

'What do you suggest we do?' Babs chewed her lip.

'We could call the police, but it would

be a difficult one to explain. I mean it's not as if Hannah was expecting you.'

'She'd never go out of an evening and leave Lucy on her own.'

'Try Hannah's mobile number again,' Xan urged.

Babs dialled the number. They both stared at each other in mounting horror as they heard the ring tone inside the house.

'Looks like she hasn't got it with her,' Xan said.

'She never goes anywhere without it,' Babs replied.

'Then we had better contact the police,' Xan said in a grim voice. 'If anything's happened to Lucy, I don't know what I'll do.'

12

'We'd like to keep her in until the morning,' the doctor informed Hannah.

Hannah raised her eyes from a now quietly sleeping Lucy. Steve had been forced to stay in the waiting room, as he wasn't a relative, leaving Hannah to deal with the doctor on her own.

'Just as a precaution,' the doctor advised.

'What was wrong with her?' Hannah asked.

'I suppose the easiest way to explain it would be to say her immune system couldn't cope with all the excitement of the day. I see from my notes you told the nurse she twisted her ankle in a sudden rainstorm and that she'd lost her jumper on the beach?'

'Yes,' Hannah replied.

'With the heat of the car and everything else, her temperature would probably have been all over the place. That's why she reacted when you put her to bed. She'll rally but it would be best to leave her here overnight. You can collect her in the morning. Children are amazingly resilient. One moment you think there's something seriously wrong with them and the next they are up and dancing.' He checked his bleeper. 'Sorry. I have to go.'

A nurse appeared.

'Can I stay with Lucy?' Hannah asked.

'Why don't you go home?' she suggested. 'And get some sleep. You're going to need it when this young lady wakes up.'

'But she won't know where she is or what's happened to her,' Hannah protested. 'I have to stay.'

'I'll stay with her.'

Hannah spun round at the sound of Ronnie's voice behind her. Falling into her sister's arms, it was all Hannah could do not to weep on her shoulder.

'Xan got a message to me,' Ronnie explained.

'I'm sorry,' the nurse interrupted,

'only relatives are allowed in.'

'I'm Lucy's mother,' Ronnie explained with her gentle smile. 'I know I look outrageous and you've every right to be concerned.' She glanced down at her muddied denim skirt. 'But I've been on the back of a motorbike. It was the only transport available at short notice and I had to get to see my daughter.'

Hannah watched her sister's smile work its magic on the nurse. 'I'll bring you a cup of tea, shall I?' offered the nurse as she drew the curtains around Lucy's bed.

'That would be brilliant.' Ronnie squeezed Hannah's hand. 'I'm sorry I wasn't here for you, and we've got so much to catch up on, but I think you'd better get outside.'

'Why?'

'Steve's in the waiting room and he's trying to deal with Xan and Mum. I think there's a situation brewing.'

'Mum's here?' Hannah was horrified at the thought of the fuss her mother would make.

'It's a long story, but she and Xan called the police. Off you go, and good luck.'

Trying not to rush out of the darkened ward at breakneck speed, Hannah blinked as the bright lights of the waiting room temporarily dazzled her. A trio of faces turned towards her and there was no mistaking Steve's relief at the sight of her.

Her mother moved forward and smothered her in kisses. 'My baby. Thank heavens you're safe.'

Out of the corner of her eye Hannah saw a shadow move in the background. She realised, to her consternation, that it was a policeman.

'If there's nothing more, madam?' he intervened, putting away his notebook.

'You've been absolutely marvellous.' Babs swept round to face him and for one awful moment Hannah thought she was going to kiss the constable too. 'I'm so sorry for all the trouble I've caused. Do you have children?'

'Two, madam.'

'Then you'll appreciate how I feel, won't you?'

Still looking bemused, the policeman took his leave.

'Hi, darlin'.' Xan ambled over. His bushy beard tickled Hannah's ear as he kissed her. 'How's it going? That's a beautiful shiner you've got there.'

'We haven't time for all that now,' Babs asserted her authority on the situation.

'You'd better have a word with Steve,' Xan murmured in Hannah's ear. 'Poor chap nearly got arrested for abuse.'

'Why?'

'Something to do with a domestic? Don't let me keep you.' He smiled and flicked a finger under her chin. 'Thanks again for all you did for Lucy. You're a star.'

'Steve?' Hannah moved towards him.

'Let's get out of here,' he said. His jaw was so tight she could barely see his lips move.

'Wait for me,' Babs called out behind them. 'They won't let more than two relatives stay with a patient and I haven't got a lift home. I came on the back of Xan's bike,' she explained.

'Is it all right,' Hannah asked Steve, 'if my mother comes with us?'

'And what if I said no?' he asked with a weary smile.

Hannah flushed. 'It is a bit of an imposition,' she admitted.

'Nonsense.' Babs gathered up her bag. 'I can sleep in Lucy's bed. Now come on. We've entertained these good folk long enough. Bye everybody.'

Several hands were waved in acknowledgement of Babs's departure. Hannah had forgotten quite how much of a whirlwind effect her mother had on strangers. She could imagine her antics would have been far more entertaining than the drama being enacted on the television screen in a corner of the room.

'It's quite a walk to the car,' Steve said, 'but the only parking space I could get was way over the back.'

Babs stifled a yawn. 'Goodness, what a day. The fresh air will probably wake me up. I have been on the go for hours, still suffering from jet lag I think.' She waggled her fingers at Hannah. 'What do you think of my ring?'

Hannah blinked. She had completely forgotten about her mother's marriage. 'It's lovely,' she replied automatically, 'and congratulations.'

'Thank you.' There was a trace of smugness in Babs's voice. 'I was so surprised when Hal proposed. I thought to myself I can't let him get away, he is too much of a catch.'

'Can we talk about this back home?' Steve intervened.

'Of course we can.' Babs linked her arm through his. 'Why don't I just shut up and let you lead the way?'

'That's the best idea I've heard all evening,' Steve replied with a wry look at Hannah, whose cheeks began to burn at the thought of what he must have been through.

★ ★ ★

The drive back was completed at a gentler speed than their race to the hospital. The streets were now deserted and Hannah saw from the church clock it was nearly two in the morning. Her mother kept up a constant stream of chatter from the back seat.

'Nothing's changed, has it? I saw Patricia Morris — goodness it was only yesterday. It seems like days ago. Anyway, she was agog to know all that's been going on. Then Xan took me out to visit his mother — you remember Etaine?'

'Mum.' Hannah put up a hand to stop her.

'I think you and Ronnie should now call me Babs,' she announced rather grandly.

'Anything you say,' Hannah agreed, determined not to be sidetracked. 'What I need to know is why you called the police.'

The flow of chatter stopped.

'They thought I'd kidnapped Lucy,' Steve explained, 'and when the police checked round the hospitals the nurse in charge here told them she was suspicious about us because you had a black eye and I was restraining you by the wrists. I was lucky not to get arrested.'

'It wasn't like that at all,' Babs protested, 'but you have to understand, I was worried. Xan was too. The place was in darkness and when we rang Hannah's mobile we heard it ringing inside the house.'

'I'm surprised I got off so lightly,' Steve replied. 'You must have painted a very black picture to the police.'

'I suppose I did go a bit over the top,' Babs admitted. 'It's always been my way.'

'Don't I know it,' Steve muttered under his breath.

'Why didn't you let us know you were coming?' Hannah demanded.

'It was a last-minute decision. Jed — you remember Hal's son?' Hannah nodded. 'He said you'd lost your job at the library and that Ronnie's commune had been closed down.'

'Did he also say why he left

Deneham in such a hurry and why he took Alison Cooper with him?' Hannah asked.

Babs wriggled and looked uncomfortable. 'Can we talk about it later?' she asked with a meaningful glance at the back of Steve's head.

'It's all right, Babs,' Steve replied, 'Alison and I are no longer an item and the relationship wasn't that serious in the first place.'

'That's not the story she gave me.' Babs held up a hand. 'Anyway, it's none of my business, but I had to come over and check things out here before I go back home.' She stifled a laugh. 'Fancy me referring to Texas as home. You must come and visit, Hannah. Bring Steve with you, although I suppose you've been loads of times?'

'I haven't, no,' Steve admitted.

'Not enough mud springs for you? Hal already has an oil well so I suppose he wouldn't have need of your services.' Babs looked over her shoulder. 'Back at last,' she said. 'Funny how the house doesn't look as menacing in the moonlight as it did earlier.'

The gravel driveway of Highworth House crunched under their tyres as Steve drove up to the front door.

'Why don't you and Babs go inside while I garage the car?'

'Are you hungry?' Hannah asked.

'Starving,' he admitted. 'It's been hours since lunch and that was only an ice cream. Can you fix something?'

'I'll see what I can do,' Babs offered, 'to make amends.'

Babs turned on the kitchen light and shrieked. 'What have you been doing?' An odour of burnt toast pervaded the atmosphere. 'And what on earth is that in the sink?' Babs picked up the congealed saucepan of baked beans.

'We were making supper when we realised Lucy was unwell,' Steve said.

'Do you have any eggs?' Babs asked.

'In the fridge.'

'Then I suggest you leave me to make the omelettes while you freshen up. Go on.' She pushed Hannah out of the kitchen. 'I was housekeeper here before your time, remember? I think I can still find my way around Steve's kitchen.'

Hannah stumbled up the stairs. Behind her she heard the murmur of voices and her mother ordering Steve to have a shower. By the time she came down the kitchen was a haven of efficiency. The work surfaces gleamed. Babs had emptied the washing machine and their laundry was now airing around the boiler that hummed comfortingly in the far corner.

For all her mother's scatty ways, Babs could also cook a mean omelette, and Hannah's mouth watered at the sight of the fluffy eggs her mother was beating up in a large bowl. The table had been laid for three.

'Help yourself.' Babs nodded towards the jug of orange juice in the centre. 'I found a chunk of cheese and some herbs which I think had been left over from my day.' She smiled. 'So it's all gone into the omelette. I unearthed a bag of apples in the cupboard, so if there's any cheese left over that'll do for dessert.'

'I'm afraid we haven't got any bread. The toaster jammed,' Hannah said.

'So I realised when I tried to clear it out. Never mind. There's more than enough here to satisfy our appetites and we don't want to eat anything too heavy before we go to bed. How long do you think Steve's going to be?'

'I've no idea. Do you want me to give him a call?'

Babs drew out a chair. 'Not just yet.' She sat down opposite her daughter. The clear blue eyes inspected Hannah's face. 'You aren't going to like what I'm about to say.'

'Can it wait?' Hannah asked. 'I think I've had my fill of shocks for one night.'

'I'm sure you've got room for one more.' Babs took a deep breath. 'I think Steve Talbot is the man for you.'

Hannah flushed to the roots of her hair. 'Mum, please. I mean Babs,' she corrected herself.

'A mother's prerogative. It's not as if

you've had many boyfriends, and it's time you settled down. At your age I was mother to two children.'

'Can we talk about something else?'

'You do like him, don't you?'

'Yes, but if we're into plain speaking, with you for a mother and Ronnie for a sister, I don't think he'd look kindly on getting seriously involved with our family. And I have to say I can't blame him.'

'By the way, where did you get that black eye?' Babs asked. 'Steve didn't give it to you, did he?'

'Lucy lashed out when she was delirious.'

'If we had some raw steak we could use it to reduce the swelling.'

'If we had some raw steak,' a voice announced from the doorway, 'I'd be asking you to cook it for me medium rare.'

'An omelette's the best I can do.' Babs got to her feet, leaving a still blushing Hannah sitting at the table wondering exactly how much of their conversation Steve had overheard.

13

'I'll be off again in the morning,' Steve announced as they sat down to their makeshift supper.

Babs appeared to have slipped back effortlessly into her role as housekeeper as she took charge of the kitchen. She served up the omelettes, found the pepper mill and made sure Hannah and Steve both replenished their drinks before settling down at the table.

'So soon?' Babs raised an eyebrow before forking up some of her omelette.

''fraid so. I've just received a text.'

'Where are you going this time?' Hannah asked.

'Somewhere in the Pacific. I'm not too sure of the exact location. They like to play these things a bit hush-hush. I've no idea why.'

'Sounds a bit like the plans to drill round here,' Babs replied.

'I've heard nothing about that,' said Steve, adding, 'Unfortunately no one seems to believe me.'

'How do you know about it?' Hannah asked her mother.

'Xan mentioned something,' Babs said. 'I can't remember all the details.'

'Val Lawrence wanted me to mention it to Ronnie but I haven't had a chance,' Hannah said.

'It looks like she already knows.'

'Well I can't help you I'm afraid.' Steve smiled. 'Although there are certain sections of the community who seem convinced it's something to do with me.'

'My older daughter does have a point, though, wouldn't you say?' Babs leaned forward to emphasise her words.

'And what is her point exactly?' Steve asked.

'There has to be a public protest if no one's been advised what is going on.'

'Ronnie's not planning one, is she?' Hannah asked in alarm. 'A protest?'

'I don't know,' Babs admitted, 'but if there is one I intend to take part.'

Hannah's forkful of omelette slipped back onto her plate. 'You can't.'

'Why not? I'm a free citizen, and I know my rights, and I'm very good at chaining myself to railings. I've had practice. I once superglued myself to a councillor's front gate. He was such a pompous man. Do you remember, Hannah?'

'Vividly.' It was a memory Hannah would never forget. She had been at school with the councillor's daughter, a bully of a girl, and when her father was accused of manipulating a building contract to his own advantage, Babs had got wind of it. She had made the front pages standing outside his detached house on the edge of the golf course, wearing her placard and with her fingers firmly attached to his wrought-iron gates. Hannah had been forced to defend her mother's actions in the playground. As a result she had gained reluctant support from some of the harder crowd for standing up to the school bully, and she supposed she should be grateful to her mother for teaching her a valid lesson in life. All the same, it was an experience she would rather not have to go through again.

Steve scraped back his chair. 'I'd better make a move. Thanks for supper, Babs. Quite the best omelette I've ever tasted. I'll try not to make too much noise in the morning as I'll be leaving early.'

'I would offer to make you some toast for breakfast,' Babs smiled at him, 'but you incinerated what was left of the loaf.'

'I'll get something at the airport. Stay as long as you like, by the way,' he offered generously before adding, 'but no demonstrations on my property, OK?'

'Understood, and thank you for what you did for Lucy tonight,' Babs said in a softer voice. 'I know the Lavender family is a trying lot, but I really am grateful, and I know I speak for my older daughter as well.'

'No worries.' Steve sketched a wave. 'Bye, Hannah.' He smiled at the pair of them and left the kitchen.

'I suppose we'd better get our heads

down too.' Babs began to clear the table. 'It's been a long day.'

'How long are you staying for?' Hannah enquired as she squirted washing-up liquid on the dirty plates.

'I do need to get back to Hal,' Babs admitted, 'but I haven't had a chance to see my granddaughter yet. Maybe I could take her away for a day or two while Ronnie sorts herself out?'

'Has Ronnie found somewhere to live?' Hannah asked.

'She's been staying with some friends in Hampshire but it was only a temporary arrangement.'

'It wouldn't be fair to ask Steve to put her up.'

'I agree,' Babs replied, 'but I don't think Ronnie would accept his offer anyway. You know . . .' She paused. 'I have the beginning of an idea.'

'Not another one.' Hannah felt a qualm of concern.

'I think I know where she can stay, and it would be in Deneham.' Babs hung up the tea towel. 'Leave it to me to make a few enquiries. I'll finish up here. Now off you go to bed.'

By the time Hannah woke the next morning the sun was streaming through her open window. The sound of the radio in the kitchen lured her downstairs after a quick shower. Her mother was sitting on the back doorstep, taking in the sun. Hannah inhaled the smell of freshly roasted coffee beans percolating.

'Darling.' Babs leapt to her feet. 'There you are. I was about to call you. Did you sleep well?'

To her surprise, Hannah had crashed out the moment her head had touched the pillow. 'It's nearly midday,' she gasped. 'Why didn't you wake me earlier?'

'No need. Anyway, it gave me time to order fresh food supplies online.' Babs indicated an impressive array of fruit and vegetables in the rack. 'I explained it was an emergency. They were ever so kind and put us on the top of the delivery list, so we can have milk in our coffee and toast for breakfast. Look.' She brandished an electrical implement in the air. 'They even delivered a new toaster. I threw the old one out. Heavens knows what Steve had been doing to it, but I'm amazed you weren't both poisoned. It was a dreadful old thing. I've been on to the hospital and Lucy's fine. She's been released and I've made arrangements for them all to stay at the Willows.'

Hannah collapsed into one of the pine kitchen chairs while her mother chattered on.

'I mean, it's the least she could do, isn't it, after all the trouble she's caused? I only had to make the teensiest hint about super glue and Patricia Morris was all agreement.'

Hannah blinked at Babs, then seizing her chance to interrupt demanded, 'You persuaded Mrs Morris to offer accommodation to Ronnie, Xan and Lucy at her house?'

'Isn't that what I just said?' Babs flicked the switch on the toaster.

'I don't see the connection to super-glue.'

'Patti did. She was a friend of the

famous councillor and she's not a fool. She knows there's a strong contingent in town that blame her for all the fuss over the commune. The last thing she wants is someone making an issue out of it.'

'That's blackmail,' Hannah protested, her sympathies entirely with Patricia Morris.

'It will only be for a few days. Xan's due to take off again for a festival or something, and you know what Ronnie's like. It won't be long before she falls out with old Patti and we'll be back to square one, but anyway for the moment things are nicely fixed up. The Willows can accommodate them all.'

The ringing of the telephone interrupted Babs.

'That'll be Hal. I left a message for him to call me back. He was out attending to one of the horses. There's marmalade and butter for your toast, so make sure you eat a proper breakfast.' Babs went out into the hall, closing the door behind her, leaving a bemused Hannah wondering how her mother had managed to achieve so much in such a short space of time.

Her own mobile leapt into life from where Hannah had left it on the windowsill.

'Everything OK?' It was Steve.

'Absolutely fine. Babs has got us a new toaster and I'm about to have breakfast.'

'Lucky you. Wish I could join you,' Steve replied. 'I'm stuck at the airport, facing a three-hour flight delay. Anyway, no more problems at your end?'

'For the moment,' was Hannah's guarded reply.

'I should be back in about a week's time,' Steve explained. 'I can't leave a contact number because I'll be travelling all over the place, and I'm told the mobile signal where I'm going is non-existent.'

In the background Hannah heard a tannoy announcement.

'I've got to go,' Steve said. 'The boss is waving at me. Looks like we could be off. Take care.'

As Hannah finished the call there was a cry behind her and a pair of excited arms was circled around her waist.

'Hannah,' Lucy squealed, 'I've got such a lot to tell you.'

'Let her breathe, Lucy Lockett.' Ronnie crowded into the kitchen behind her. 'I need to speak to Han first.'

'I'm going to look at my vegetable garden. There'll be ever such a lot to do.' Lucy picked out a banana from the fruit bowl, then raced out of the back door.

'I see Mum's been busy.' Without asking for permission, Ronnie poured herself some coffee and crammed two more slices of bread into the toaster.

'We have to call her Babs now,' Hannah replied, wishing she could look as effortlessly knockout as her sister. Ronnie was wearing her trademark sunhat, a yellow T-shirt and peasant skirt. Hannah looked down at her own sensible blouse and trousers and sighed.

'Babs it is then,' Ronnie replied.

'Where's Xan?'

'Tinkering with his beloved bike. Said it was running too rich or something.' Ronnie's hand was warm as she reached across the table and clutched Hannah's arm. 'Thanks, Han, for everything.'

Hannah shook her head. 'Not necessary.' A lump lodged in her throat. 'It was my fault Lucy caught cold. She was so ill afterwards I was really scared.'

'That's not how my daughter tells it. She said she had a wonderful day eating ice cream, talking to the crab man as she calls him, then chasing dogs on the beach, before waking up in a hospital bed to find me and Xan sitting beside her.'

'She twisted her ankle so badly she couldn't walk. Then she got a fever. She was delirious, Ronnie.'

'That's kids for you. Wait until you have some of your own.' Hannah scraped butter onto her toast and coated it liberally with marmalade. 'So, have you managed to learn anything about this proposed drilling site?'

'Only what Val Lawrence told me.'

Hannah quickly related Val's story about a scout.

'Sounds pretty much the same story I've heard. Does Steve still maintain it's nothing to do with him?'

'He said so last night.'

'Then that man is not telling the truth.'

'How do you know?' Hannah gasped.

'My sources say the reason he bought this house was because it would make a convenient headquarters from which he could conduct operations.'

'I don't believe it.'

'Neither did I at first, but I've got irrefutable evidence.'

'What sort of evidence?'

'Letters, emails.'

'You haven't hacked into his account, have you?'

'With my computer skills?' Ronnie laughed and brushed breadcrumbs off her T-shirt. 'If you must know, Alison Cooper told me.'

'She's back?'

'And she means business.'

'Is Jed back too?'

'Don't think so.'

Hannah debated briefly whether or not to mention her mother's mistrust of her stepson, but before she could say anything Babs swept into the kitchen.

'Darling.' She air-kissed Ronnie. 'How are things with the divine Patti?'

'We could be in for a bumpy ride,' Ronnie admitted, 'but for the moment it's working well. Thanks for arranging it.'

'Any time.' She glanced out of the window. 'Heavens, what is that child doing? I'd better rescue her before she digs a hole to Australia.'

'Babs mentioned a possible protest. You weren't thinking of Highworth House, were you?' Hannah voiced her worst fears to Ronnie.

'Where better? Xan told me our banners are in the garage, nice and handy. All we have to do is rally the troops and we're in business.'

'You can't do that to Steve.'

'Why not?'

'He's done so much for you. If it hadn't been for him, heaven knows what would have happened to Lucy.'

'I know, Han, and I'm grateful, but this demonstration won't be about personal issues. There's a wider cause.'

'You promised there wouldn't be any protests here.'

'And there won't be.'

'You just said there would.'

'We'll be outside the gates and there's no law in the land that can stop us using the public highway for the purpose.'

'Are you sure?'

Ronnie took a healthy bite out of her toast. Hannah knew she had asked a silly question. Ronnie was totally up to speed when it came to this sort of thing. For the first time in her life, Hannah felt she wanted nothing more to do with her sister.

14

As had been the case with the dismantling of the commune, the demonstration was swiftly arranged. For someone who had left school under a cloud and professing no interest in anything academic, the standard of Ronnie's organisational skills was seriously professional. Hannah was still reeling from the shock of hearing Ronnie's plans when an excited Lucy raced into the kitchen.

'Mummy,' she squealed, 'there's a van covered in purple daisies parked in the drive. It's playing ever such loud music, and Nana's helping the driver load the banns into the back.'

'The what?' Hannah raised her voice above the bass thumps emanating from the boom box.

'She means the banners, don't you, Lucy Lockett,' Ronnie explained with a wide smile at her daughter.

'Why are the banners being loaded onto the van?' Hannah asked.

'Because I didn't think it was fair to use Steve's storage space any longer. I do have some scruples,' Ronnie laughed.

Lucy tugged at Hannah's sleeve. 'Come and see.'

Outside, the decibel level was shattering. 'Will you please turn the music off?' Hannah yelled to the driver.

'Sorry,' he apologised, 'I like my heavy metal loud.'

'Thank you,' Hannah said in a chilly voice.

'I think that's the lot.' Babs finished directing the operation with an efficiency Ronnie seemed to have inherited. She emerged from behind several pots of paint with a cheerful smile. 'All sorted,' she advised her daughters, brushing cobwebs off her kaftan and running her fingers through her hair. 'Would anybody like a cool drink?'

'Yay!' Lucy danced a jig in the forecourt. 'Orange for me please, Nana.'

'Nigel?' Babs asked the van driver.

'Don't gape, Han. It's rude,' Ronnie rebuked her. 'Although I have to admit, the first time I realised his name was Nigel I gaped too. I mean — ' Her brown eyes danced with amusement. ' — he's lovely, but I thought Nigels were accountants, not tattooed leather-jacketed Goths.'

'Then you really are going ahead with this demonstration?' Hannah felt sick in the pit of her stomach.

'We are,' Ronnie affirmed. 'I would tell you when it's all going to happen, Han, only I think you'd sneak the details to Steve.'

'I'd best be going, Ronnie.' Nigel declined Babs's offer of a drink. 'See you later, guys.' He climbed back into his van and rattled out of the drive.

'I'd like you all to leave now.' Hannah crossed her arms in a gesture of confrontation.

'Darling,' Babs objected, 'Ronnie's only just arrived.'

'You too, Babs. Didn't you mention something about taking Lucy away for a few days?'

'Yes I did, but I hadn't made any plans.'

'Then I suggest you start now. None of you are welcome here any longer.'

'Darling.' Babs frowned. 'What's the matter?'

'Han?' Ronnie, too, looked upset.

'Do I have to leave as well?' Lucy's lower lip trembled.

Hannah confronted the trio of faces. It was always like this. As long as she went along with their plans they were sweetness and light, but the moment she put her foot down they ganged up on her. It didn't matter how outrageously they were behaving, she was expected to toe the family line. She supported all of them as much as she could, but enough was enough. She had reached the end of her tether.

'Can't you see how embarrassing this is for me? And Ronnie, I'm ashamed of you. Where were you when Lucy was ill? I had no one to turn to except Steve. He was the only one there for me, and this how you repay him for his kindness.'

'Han.' Ronnie held out her hand. 'I understand, really I do, but there are always casualties of war. Steve falls into that category.'

'Don't be so ridiculous.' Hannah tossed her head. She could feel the back of her throat tightening. 'All you have to do is call off your demonstration and there wouldn't be any so-called war.'

'I can't do that.'

'Then you'll understand why you're no longer welcome here.'

'Why are you and Aunty Hannah arguing, Mummy?' Lucy asked.

'Why don't we go and look at your vegetables?' Babs suggested to her granddaughter.

'I don't want to. You promised me a drink of orange.'

'Then we'll go and get one in the kitchen. Sort it out, girls,' she said over Lucy's head, 'but quietly please. We can't have the little one upset.'

Hannah's chest heaved as she glared at Ronnie. In all her years of protesting she had never felt like this before about her sister. 'Steve's told you it's absolutely nothing to do with him, not once, but on numerous occasions. Why won't you believe him?'

'Because I've been told otherwise.'

'By Alison Cooper? Can't you see she's stirring things up for her own ends?'

'I don't think so.'

'Why do you believe her and not Steve?'

'What she tells me holds the ring of truth.'

'In that case you'll have to excuse me if I say I don't believe you.'

'Han, what's the matter with you?'

'You believe Alison without giving Steve a chance to deny the accusation. What happened to the freedom marches and the protest songs decrying the rights of the individual? What rights are you giving Steve?'

'Very good, Han.' Ronnie nodded approvingly. 'Are you sure I can't recruit you?'

Hannah clenched her fists. 'I want you to call this whole thing off.'

'I've already told you, I can't.'

'How can you be so stubborn?'

'People are coming from all over the country. It's too late to stop them now.'

'You should have spoken to me first before you started on this nonsense.'

'Now hold on, Han.'

'It was because of Alison that I lost my job here.'

'I know that, Han, and wasn't it me who offered you shelter when you had no one else to turn to?'

Hannah began to feel out of her depth. Ronnie could always turn a situation to her own advantage.

'She went off with Jed Beckett in an attempt to make Steve jealous. When that didn't work, she's decided to stir up more trouble by spinning tales about him that aren't true, and you've fallen neatly into her trap. You disappoint me, Ronnie. I thought better of you. Up until now I believed in you. You know your trouble? You're beginning to believe your own publicity. You've forgotten your principles.'

'I think you're right, Han,' Ronnie admitted after a short silence. 'We should cool things between us for a while. I don't want to argue with you, and if we carry on like this, before long one of us is going to say something we might regret.'

'I never took you for a fool, Ronnie,' Hannah called after her, 'but this time what you're doing is morally wrong.'

Lucy ran over to kiss Hannah goodbye. 'Nana and I are going to visit Nana Etaine in the woods.'

'Don't worry, darling.' Babs hugged her daughter. 'We've got somewhere proper to sleep over. You know how Lucy is with animals, so we thought we'd take in a theme park and have a bit of girl-time together. It may be a while before I get another chance to have my grand-daughter to myself.'

'What about the demonstration?' Hannah asked.

'Best not talk about that right now I think, don't you? Try to make it up with Ronnie. I know she can be wilful at times, but she is your sister.'

Why did her mother always make it sound as though Hannah were at fault? She fumed. Ronnie and Babs were twin souls. They understood each other. Hannah made allowances for their differences in character, but not this time. She was never speaking to Ronnie again.

The house was quiet after Babs had packed up and left with Lucy. Hannah sat down at the kitchen table and tried to think things through. Should she tell Steve of Ronnie's plan if he telephoned, or should she hope the whole thing would blow over before he came home?

And what of Jed Beckett? No one else seemed to have linked him with the drilling project. If only she knew where Alison was, she could confront her face to face.

A quiet tap on the back door startled her. 'Hello, dear, sorry, didn't mean to interrupt.'

'Mrs Morris?' She stared at the woman in surprise. 'If you're looking for Ronnie I'm afraid she's not here. In fact, I'm not sure where she is.'

'It's you I came to speak to actually. Do you mind if I sit down? Is it all right if I let Harlequin off his lead? Out you go.' She shooed the dog into the garden. 'Don't worry, he won't cause any trouble.'

Hannah waited patiently while Mrs Morris settled down. 'What can I do for you?' she asked.

'Have you heard about Ronnie's plans for a demonstration?'

'Steve isn't anything to do with these proposed plans.' Hannah was growing tired of repeating herself.

'What exactly is going on?' Mrs Morris asked. 'No one will tell me.'

'There's been a rumour doing the rounds that one of the big conglomerates is looking for a drilling site to run tests for natural resources. Steve is in the firing line because of the nature of his work. He denies it's anything to do with him but no one seems to be listening.'

'If only I hadn't interfered. I only registered a mild complaint, but the next thing I knew the field was empty.'

'Do you realise the trouble you've caused?'

'If there's anything I can do,' Mrs Morris pleaded, 'please don't hesitate to ask. I offered Ronnie temporary accommodation but she wants to move on. I've had a word with Farmer Tony but he won't give permission for the commune to return to the field with all this other trouble hanging over his head.'

'I think you've done more than enough,' Hannah replied in a cold voice.

'If I can, I'll try to get the march stopped, but I don't think my influence holds much sway.' Mrs Morris hesitated. 'There is one thing I can offer you, however,' she said slowly.

'What's that?' Hannah asked.

'A room. If things should go badly with Mr Talbot as a result of all this talk of demonstrations, please don't hesitate

207

to come to me. I really am very sorry and I'd like to make amends.'

'Thank you for the offer, Mrs Morris.' It was difficult to be polite but Hannah was determined not to lose her dignity. 'I'll bear it in mind.'

'The library hasn't been the same without you. I've been reduced to listening to Jim Matthews spin on about the old days, and you have to be desperate to do that. I do miss our little chats.'

When Hannah didn't respond Patricia took the hint.

'Call me any time, day or night. These days my time is my own,' she said a trifle wistfully. 'I'd like a bit of company, so you needn't feel it's an imposition. I've lots of spare space.'

Harlequin pattered into the kitchen, leaving a trail of muddy paw marks on the floor. 'Where have you been?' Patricia demanded. 'Look at that mess. No — ' She grabbed the floor mop off Hannah. ' — I'll do it. In fact, if there are any other little jobs you'd like me to help out with — ?'

Hannah relented. She began to realise that Patricia Morris had only poked her nose into other people's business because she was lonely. 'I do need some shopping. Perhaps you'd drive me into town?'

'On the way we'll stop somewhere for lunch, shall we? That is, unless you've already eaten?'

Hannah looked down at the remains of her uneaten breakfast.

'Why don't I clear up here while you go and get your bag? Go on,' Mrs Morris urged. 'A breath of fresh air will do us both good, and you never know — between us we may be able to come up with a plan to counter this demonstration. I really did mean what I said. I'll do anything to help.'

Stumbling up the stairs, Hannah marvelled at yet another strange turn her life had taken. She now had an ally in Patricia Morris, and between them it might be possible to halt the demonstration before things went too far.

15

Hannah cowered behind the curtains. Things were turning out worse than she had imagined. It had been a while since she had seen Ronnie in action, and she had really gone to town. She appeared to have rounded up every able-bodied activist in the country. Even with the windows firmly closed, Hannah could hear them chanting.

'Out, out, out!' they roared, waving banners in the air. Hannah peered through a chink in the curtains and was confronted by a sea of slogans. Bright red paint had been daubed on cardboard placards and they were being brandished aloft on sticks. Nearly every protester was wearing a vivid orange T-shirt over-printed in bright green lettering with the slogan, 'Out, Out, Out'. Someone was playing a flute and someone else was banging a drum.

Together the protesters linked arms and swayed to the music.

Large vans were parked down the lane and Hannah could make out some trailing cables and several earnest-looking reporters thrusting microphones under people's noses. Some protesters had come in fancy dress. One man was juggling a set of brightly coloured balls and another was dressed as a scarecrow. A team of young girls was twirling hula-hoops, and another group was performing a dance. Hannah would have enjoyed the spectacle and the carnival atmosphere of the occasion if it hadn't been for such an unpleasant purpose.

At the back of her mind she still couldn't help suspecting that Ronnie had been manipulated. Her sister had a keen mind and if she had looked at the situation logically, she would have realised that maybe there was a lot more going on here than a demonstration against an innocent member of the public.

Hannah's teeth dented her lower lip as she stared in horrified fascination at the goings-on at the end of Steve's drive. Arc lights had been erected and a man in a sharp suit with a brush haircut was broadcasting a running commentary on the activities.

Hannah was now beginning to wish she had mentioned the proposed trouble to Steve, but things had gone quiet after her disagreement with Ronnie and Hannah and she had hoped it might have been a storm in a teacup. Her optimism had been sadly misplaced.

Patricia Morris had proved a good contact and made daily reports. She told Hannah she had seen and heard nothing suspicious, but she had obviously been left out of the loop.

The sound of a crowd of protesters outside Highworth House had woken Hannah that morning and she realised from the off that they meant business. She hadn't dared venture out of the house or show herself at the window. One or two of the bolder activists had tied their wrists to the gates and despite police persuasion refused to budge.

Hannah squinted at the sea of faces. There was no sign of Ronnie. She didn't want to panic, but the situation was looking more serious by the minute. A loud ring on the doorbell made her jump. She tensed. Before she could decide whether or not to answer it, the bell rang again.

'Who is it?' she called through the letterbox.

'The police, madam. May we come in?'

'Can I see your identity first?' she asked, well versed in the subterfuges some of the lesser principled protesters adopted to enter a property.

Two warrant cards were thrust through the slot and Hannah took her time checking the credentials. 'What do you want?' she asked as she slid them back.

'Can you open the door, madam? We'd like to talk to you.'

Hannah unlocked the door but kept the chain fastened. She peered round and saw two uniformed officers on the doorstep, one male and one female.

'If you wouldn't mind unlatching the chain?' the officer with the sergeant stripes asked. 'It might be quieter to talk inside. Thank you.'

The two of them sidled through the gap as Hannah released the door a fraction. 'What is going on?' she demanded.

'A group of protesters have an issue with the owner of this property — ' One of the officers consulted his notebook. ' — who is I believe a Mr Talbot?'

'Why?'

'It's to do with ecological issues,' the younger officer intervened.

'Can't you stop them?' Hannah asked in a shrill voice.

'Not unless they gain illegal access to the property.'

'But some are chained to the gate.'

'We are doing our best to rectify the situation, but until then I would suggest you stay inside. Your appearance might inflame the situation.'

'What about my human rights? Aren't they being infringed?' Hannah demanded, not sure where she stood on that one, but it was a phrase she'd heard quoted in the past.

The police officers ignored it. 'I understand you are Mr Talbot's house-keeper and that you are here alone?' one of them asked.

Hannah nodded.

'Where is Mr Talbot?'

'In South America I think.'

The senior policeman nodded. 'We'll do our best to contain the protest, but there's often a rogue element in these types of situations.'

'They're not going to break down the gates, are they?'

'We'll make sure they don't get that far, madam.'

A bleeper crackled and a disembod-ied voice announced, 'Two suspects have superglued themselves together, Sarge.'

The sergeant raised his eyebrows. 'We'll have to go and sort that out. I think it fair to warn you that there is a media presence outside and they will be conducting interviews. They may try to contact you. I would advise you not to speak to the press if it can be avoided.'

'Do you know the names of any of the protesters?' Hannah was reluctant to ask the question, but she had to know if Ronnie was involved.

'Most of them go by the name of Smith,' was the wry reply. 'Why do you ask?'

'My sister might be amongst them.'

'And her name is?'

'Ronnie Lavender.'

'The lady isn't unknown to us,' the sergeant admitted. 'I'll try to find out if she's outside. Do you want to talk to her?'

Hannah shook her head. 'I keep telling her Steve — Mr Talbot — isn't involved in these ecological issues, as she calls them. We had a disagreement over it and — ' She shrugged. ' — we haven't spoken since.'

'Is there any message you'd like me to pass on?'

'Tell her to stop this protest.' Hannah raised her voice in agitation. 'It won't do any good.'

'We'll try our best, madam,' the younger police officer assured her. 'If you do have any trouble then this is the number to contact.'

'You mean like bricks through the window?' Hannah asked.

'It shouldn't come to that, and once they've had their five minutes of publicity I'm sure the fuss will all die down.'

'What do I do in the meantime?'

'Sit it out, I'm afraid.'

Hannah closed the door behind the policemen, her heart beating so fast she could hardly breathe. The telephone began to ring. Hannah decided not to answer it.

'Hello?' The message recorder clicked in. 'Hannah, are you there?'

'Babs?' Hannah snatched up the receiver at the sound of her mother's voce. 'Where are you?'

'Outside the house.'

'I can't let you in. The police have advised me to stay put and I daren't activate the electronic switch on the gates in case everyone swarms up the drive.'

'That's all right, dear. I don't want to come in. I'm part of the demonstration.'

'You're what?'

'Don't worry, I won't let things get out of control, but we must make a stand.'

'Against what?'

'We have to guard the countryside for future generations.'

'Steve's onside with that one. You know that.'

'I called to say I'm about to record an interview for the lunchtime news. Why don't you turn your television on?'

Hannah grabbed the remote control and flicked to the news channel. Her mother's face swam into focus. She appeared to be wearing one of her brighter coloured kaftans and was smiling at the camera.

'Mrs Beckett?' A microphone was thrust under nose.

'Babs, please.'

'Babs, I understand your daughter is one of the architects of today's demonstration.'

'We both feel strongly about the environment, and we don't want the countryside desecrated, and we're both prepared to make a stand. Someone has to guard the heritage for future generations. I have a granddaughter and I want her to be able to enjoy the countryside, not sit having a picnic on a roadside watching machinery desecrate the natural habitat of our wildlife as yet another green field is turned into a concrete jungle.'

'Why have you chosen this site to make your protest?'

'Because we believe the person living here knows about the plans to start researching this area, drilling and all the rest of it.'

Babs waved her banner enthusiastically, the protesters cheered, and the camera spanned the frontage of Highworth House.

Hannah felt sick and wished she had the nerve to race down the drive and grab the microphone from the reporter and have her say. How could her mother come out with such outrageous things?

'That's not true,' a voice rang out.

Hannah's eyes widened as a scuffle followed the interruption and the interviewer swung away from her mother to confront the newcomer.

'I happen to know for a fact that the scout responsible for searching out suitable sites in this area was none other than this lady's stepson, Jed Beckett.'

A poised Alison Cooper smiled confidently at the camera. The crowd fell silent. Hannah could now hear every word.

'I think it's an outrage that this demonstration should take place outside my fiancé's house. I've appraised him of the situation and he will be flying home immediately, cutting short an important contract. He is a committed member of the community and is extremely disappointed that lady who is his ex-housekeeper and her daughter, who arranged this demonstration, should think otherwise. What is more — ' Alison raised her voice, although it was no longer necessary. ' — when Mrs Beckett left my fiancé's employ without giving notice, she locked him out of his own house. Despite all that, he was kind enough to offer the position of housekeeper to her younger daughter because she had had recently lost her job. That doesn't sound like an uncaring member of the community, does it? He also looked after Mrs Beckett's granddaughter when she was ill, driving her to the hospital and staying with her until contact could be made with her mother, who was off on one of her jaunts. And this is how the family thanks him.'

'It wasn't like that,' Babs protested, but no one was listening.

'I myself came across Jed Beckett in my fiancé's kitchen. He was holding hands with this lady's younger daughter.' Alison was on a roll. 'There is no way she can deny her family's involvement in this disgraceful incident. I demand that the authorities take appropriate action.'

The camera swung back to where an outraged Ronnie was superglued to another protester and unable to move, then over to where Babs was gaping like a goldfish.

The interviewer was going into overdrive. 'This latest development has thrown a new light on the proceedings,' she began.

Sickened by the events, Hannah was unable to watch any more of the unfolding debacle. She turned off the television. Every word Alison Cooper had said was true, except perhaps the bit about being engaged to Steve, but for all Hannah knew they had rekindled their romance. The telephone began ringing again.

'Hannah?' she now heard Steve's voice calling her name. 'Pick up the phone; I know you're there. I have to talk to you.'

Ignoring his plea, Hannah climbed the stairs to her room. She didn't want to be around when Steve got back. He would never want to see her or any member of her family again, and right now neither did Hannah. She began throwing things into her suitcase.

16

Hannah hammered on the front door knocker. It was shaped like a goldfish and the brightly polished brass glinted in the afternoon sunlight.

'Go away!' a muffled voice shouted at her as a dog began to bark. 'Be quiet, Harlequin.'

'Patricia? Are you there? It's me.'

'Hannah?'

'Let me in.'

There was the sound of a key turning and an anxious face peered around the door. 'For goodness sake, what are you doing on my doorstep?'

'Can I stay?' Hannah held up a hastily packed suitcase.

'Are you on your own?' Patricia glanced over Hannah's shoulder.

'I had to cut through the back way but I'm not sure if I was seen.'

'Your poor child.' Patricia dragged

her through the door and slammed it shut behind her. 'Those dreadful reporters have been going up and down the cul-de-sac trying to get the residents to give an interview for their ghastly television programmes. Sorry to sound so rude, but I thought you were one of them. Of course you can stay as long as you like, dear, and you needn't worry about bumping into your sister. I've sent her packing. I didn't like turning her out, but after what she did to poor Mr Talbot — then blaming me for starting it all and making me a scapegoat — well I have to say I didn't mince my words. I told her exactly what I thought of her underhand tactics, and that she wasn't welcome here anymore. It's got so bad, I dare not show my face in town. Leave your things in the hall. We'll have a cup of tea to revive our spirits and you can update me on the latest. I haven't been outside the door all day.'

Hannah followed Patricia through to her sunlit kitchen.

'Has Steve Talbot dismissed you again?' Patricia bustled around looking for milk and teabags.

Hannah perched on a stool by the breakfast bar and did her best to catch her breath. 'I didn't give him the chance,' she admitted, wishing the heavy lump of heartache in the pit of her stomach would dissolve. She knew there was no point in waiting around to hear what he had to say. He wouldn't believe her side of the story, and in his shoes she had to admit she would feel the same.

'I saw that girlfriend of his being interviewed on the news. She really put the cat among the pigeons, didn't she? She's another one I wouldn't trust as far as I could throw her. I notice she left out the bit about her relationship with Jed Beckett. Help yourself to the biscuits.' Patricia's voice drew her back to the present.

Hannah chewed absently on a coconut cookie. Her stomach churned. She hadn't eaten anything all day but she wasn't hungry.

'So, what happened up at the house?' Patricia asked.

'Steve left a message on the answering machine saying he would be home as soon as he could,' Hannah explained. 'I asked one of the police officers to give Steve's keys to Alison and to tell her I was leaving and that she was welcome to move in.'

'You did the right thing.'

'Are you sure it's all right for me to stay?' Hannah asked. 'I couldn't think where else to go.'

'I'm glad you came. I've got enough food in the freezer to feed an army. I made extra when your sister came to stay, so we can stay holed up here for days.'

'Thank you.' Hannah gave her a shaky smile.

Patricia sat down, a puzzled look on her face. 'You know, I always thought Ronnie was a level-headed young lady.'

'So did I,' Hannah agreed.

'I can't help feeling she has been used by Alison and Jed.'

227

'Why?' Hannah asked, intrigued that Patricia's suspicions should mirror her own.

'It's not my place to say, but I should imagine Jed wanted to steer the spotlight away from himself. Things were probably getting a bit uncomfortable for him, and what with the strength of public opinion he felt it was time to take a back seat. He and Alison must have hatched a plan to point the finger of suspicion at Steve, only she did the dirty on him by exposing him.'

'Why?'

'Alison's no fool. She wanted to get back into Steve's good books and she chose her moment well, wouldn't you say? It can't have been a coincidence her turning up like that, just as your mother was being interviewed. It was a carefully orchestrated game plan.'

'Everyone seems to have been using everyone else as far as I can see,' Hannah said. 'I never realised Deneham was such a hotbed of mistrust.'

Patricia squeezed Hannah's hand in a

gesture of support.

'I did pick up a piece of gossip from Carol,' she said. 'You know Farmer Tony's wife?'

Hannah nodded.

'She told me she's heard that all planning has been shelved for now due to lack of finances. She also told me Tony was thinking about allowing the commune back. He doesn't like the field being unoccupied.'

Hannah sagged against the back of the kitchen chair and stifled a yawn.

'You poor child.' Patricia was all sympathy. 'You must be exhausted. Why don't you get some rest? Here, leave your case with me. I'll see to your laundry.'

'I couldn't let you do that,' Hannah protested.

'Nonsense. I like to feel useful. You've no idea how lonely I've been since my family left and I lost my poor dear Arthur. You can use the spare room. It's got an en suite bathroom, so have a good long soak. I'll sort out some fresh towels for you. Then what say we have a cosy supper of scrambled eggs in front of the television and take in a film? I've a nice bottle of wine somewhere too, just the thing for shattered systems.'

Hannah's throat locked. She felt embarrassed over some of the things she had in the past said about Patricia Morris. She should have realised that like Jim Matthews Patricia was lonely, only she hid her feelings behind a mask of nosiness.

'That would be lovely, and thank you, Patricia. I didn't know who to turn to.'

'That's what friends are for.' Patricia was now pink with pleasure. 'By the way, does Steve know you were coming here? I mean I can cope with him hammering on the door, but I wouldn't want Harlequin taking a bite out of his leg. My poor baby has been so upset by all this; he's very out of sorts.'

'I didn't tell anyone where I was going and I'm sure if Alison suspects where I am, she'll be the last person to tell Steve of my whereabouts.'

'Right, well off you go, dear. I'll see to supper. Come down when you're ready.'

★ ★ ★

The fuss died down over the following week and Hannah and Patricia settled into an uneasy routine, neither of them sure whether or not the protests would flare up again.

'I need to start looking for a new job,' Hannah said one afternoon after they'd finished washing up the lunch plates.

'There's no rush,' Patricia insisted.

'I can't sit around all day doing nothing.'

'What we both need is a good dose of fresh air. Why don't we grab a couple of woolly hats? We can pull them down over our hair.'

'Why?' Hannah asked, perplexed.

'As a disguise. We don't want to be recognised. We can take Harelquin for a long walk. We're all in need of some exercise and I refuse to be held hostage any longer in my own house.'

Suitably hatted, and with their coat collars turned up, the two women and Harlequin headed out across the common after they'd checked there was no evidence of camera crews still lurking in the close. The only evidence of the recent media presence was one flattened protest banner on the grass verge. Patricia threw it into her recycling bin with a disgusted sigh. 'Come on, Hannah. Let's get going,' she said as she rubbed her dirty hands down the side of her wax jacket.

They climbed to the top of the hill overlooking the golf course. 'It's one of my favourite walks,' Patricia puffed as they reached the summit. 'I come up here quite often. I find it clears my head.'

Hannah took some deep breaths. The soft grass swished against their boots and a brisk breeze whipped up colour in their cheeks.

'You're looking better already,' Patricia

said, surveying the view below them. 'It all looks so peaceful, doesn't it? It's difficult to believe Deneham was the centre of such frenzied media activity only a few days ago.'

'Do you think I ought to contact Steve?' Hannah asked. 'I mean, I did walk out on him and he does deserve an explanation. I won't tell him where I am.'

'I didn't like to mention it earlier,' Patricia began.

'He's been in touch with you?'

'No, nothing like that. There's a picture of him on the front of this week's local paper, arm in arm with Alison. She's smiling at the camera, very much the heroine of the hour. There was an in-depth interview but I didn't bother to read it. I can guess what it said.'

Hannah stifled down the sharp stab of pain in her ribs. Steve had showed her nothing but kindness even if he had in the beginning forced her to work for him. She would have liked to say she was sorry that things hadn't worked out and to wish him well for the future. She supposed now she wouldn't get the chance.

Patricia gave a self-conscious smile. 'Your relationship with Steve Talbot is absolutely none of my business, dear. And I know they say there's only one thing to do with good advice, and that's to ignore it, but my mother had a saying that has proved itself repeatedly: things generally sort themselves out, so give it time.'

Hannah opened her mouth to speak, but before she could she caught sight of a figure striding purposefully up the hill towards them. Her colourful coat was bright pink and she wore a tartan hat with a feather sticking out of it.

'Darlings,' she greeted them. 'I've been looking everywhere for you.'

Hannah stiffened as her mother embraced her.

'Babs.' Patricia all but sniffed her greeting. 'Now you've found us, what have you to say for yourself?'

'I don't know where to start.' Babs didn't look in the least abashed by the set-down. 'I am so sorry for blaming lovely Steve for all the trouble.'

'So you should be.' Patricia was in no mood to go easy on Hannah's mother. 'You'll be lucky if he doesn't take things further, especially as the real culprit was much closer to home.'

Babs had the grace to blush. 'I had no idea Jed was the scout. You do believe me, don't you?' She turned pleading blue eyes on the pair of them. 'As for Steve, he's pleased everything's been sorted out, and now the protesters have moved on he regards the matter as closed.'

'You've talked to him?' Hannah spoke for the first time.

'I felt I had to. He was very understanding and he's promised to keep in touch after he gets back.'

'Back from where?' Hannah asked.

'I'm not too sure actually,' Babs gushed, unaware of the turmoil going on in Hannah's insides. 'You've no need to worry about the house; Alison is looking after things in his absence.' Babs pulled a face. 'She's cock-a-whoop of course, now she's back in control. I'm not so sure Steve sees it like that. Anyway,' Babs said, looking at both of them, 'where have you been hiding yourselves?'

'Since your antics made life difficult for the pair of us, we've been keeping ourselves to ourselves,' Patricia admitted.

'Where's Ronnie?' Hannah asked, 'and Lucy?' Her conscience tweaked her about the child. She was an innocent victim in all the upheaval.

'They're fine. Xan's sister has been looking after Lucy while Ronnie's been busy making plans.'

'What sort of plans?' Patricia asked, a note of caution in her voice.

'Hot off the press,' Babs trilled, 'the commune is coming back. I was actually securing a few damaged fences when I saw the pair of you tramping across the upper field. Tony says they can move back in whenever they like.' Babs cast a sideways glance at Patricia. 'I take it you have no objection?'

'Don't start on all that again,' was Patricia's brisk reply. 'But I do feel it's time Ronnie realised her responsibilities and got herself sorted out properly.'

'She told me,' Babs admitted, 'that she's thinking of going into local politics. She's going to see about standing for election.'

'Well tell her in future to be sure of her facts before she goes public,' Patricia advised.

'Did anyone explain to Steve why I left?' Hannah interrupted their conversation.

'No one knew, or if they did they weren't saying. You didn't leave a note or anything, did you?' Babs asked.

'There wasn't time.'

'To be honest, after I made my apologies to Steve I left too. I thought it best, but I'm sure he'd be glad to hear from you.'

Hannah bit down a sigh. It was

always the same with her mother. She flew in like a tornado, stirred everyone up, then managed to extricate herself without a stain on her character.

'Where are you staying?' Patricia asked Babs during the silence that fell between them.

'Up at the farm with Carol and Tony, but I'll be leaving the day after tomorrow. Time I went back to my husband.'

'How do things stand between you and Jed?' Hannah asked.

'Hal knows all about what happened here. Jed will always be his son of course, but in future his visits to the ranch will be less regular and strictly by invitation only.' Babs glanced at her watch. 'I'd best be going. I've so many things to do. Now, darling, I absolutely insist you come and visit me real soon, as the Americans say. Hal is so longing to catch up with both my girls.' Babs tucked a few stray strands of hair back into Hannah's woolly hat. 'And make things up with Ronnie?'

Hannah flinched at the mention of

her sister's name.

'I know what she did was wrong, but she is your sister and Lucy is missing you.'

Hannah was missing her niece too, but she still couldn't come to terms with how Ronnie had treated Steve.

'Bye, Patti.' Babs waved at Patricia. 'Look after my girl for me and I'll forever be in your debt.' With another cheery wave she turned away and began making her way back down the hill.

Neither Patricia nor Hannah spoke for a few minutes. Shading her eyes against the sun, Patricia saw a vehicle driving into the lower field. It was followed by a procession of other vehicles.

'I have to say they didn't waste much time,' Patricia said as she watched the occupants jump out and begin erecting temporary shelters.

Hannah shivered.

'Let's get back,' Patricia suggested. 'That wind is getting up. I'm feeling a mite chilly.'

The two women walked along in

silence. In the distance they could hear the metallic clang of tow bars being released from trailers, and laughter and voices, accompanied by the smell of something savoury being brewed on their open fire.

'Making me feel hungry,' Patricia admitted as they unlatched her back garden gate and walked down the crazy-paving path to her conservatory. 'It will be nice to have things back to normal again, won't it?'

As far as Hannah was concerned, her life would never be normal again.

17

'What do you want?' Steve held up his hand before his visitor could reply. 'Haven't you caused enough trouble in my life already?' He glared at the woman standing on his doorstep.

'I know I must be absolutely the last person you want to see at the moment,' she said, 'but I called by to say I'm sorry.'

A look of scepticism crossed Steve's face.

'I'd like to explain what happened.'

'I know exactly what happened.' Steve glanced over Ronnie's shoulder. 'Where's Lucy?'

'I left her with Etaine, Xan's mother. They're going to go for a walk this afternoon to see how many birds they can spot in the woods.'

'And your mother?'

'Safely back Stateside.'

'I'm pleased to hear it.'

'I'm on my own, so may I come in?'

Steve opened the door wider to allow Ronnie to pass.

'I note you didn't ask about Hannah.' A dimple dented Ronnie's cheek as she entered the hall, removing her pink straw hat and running her fingers through her hair. Ignoring her remark about Hannah, Steve led her through to the conservatory.

'Alison keeps a tidy house.' Ronnie looked around approvingly at the neat piles of magazines and freshly watered pot plants. Lemon-scented polish lingered in the air, and all the visible surfaces were dust-free.

'Alison is no longer here. Sit down. Can I get you anything? Tea, coffee? I've even got some organic pear juice if you're interested.'

'No thank you.' Ronnie fiddled with the tassel of her jacket. 'Alison's left, you say?'

'She has.'

Ronnie could tell by the firm note in

Steve's voice that no further information would be forthcoming on Alison's whereabouts.

'I don't know where to start,' she began, changing the subject. 'I'm not used to apologising for my behaviour.'

A wry smile twisted Steve's mouth. 'I should imagine you aren't,' he agreed.

'I behaved badly and I'm sorry. Will that do?'

'For starters.'

'If my actions have caused any damage to your property, then I'd be pleased to put things right.'

'Apart from the loss of a bit of paint no harm was done to my railings, but what about your wrists?' Steve glanced down to the bruises on her flesh. 'Have you had them seen to?'

'I have,' Ronnie assured him, 'and they're healing up nicely, although it's still a bit painful to write.'

'So we can look forward to less daubs on placards?'

'For the moment,' Ronnie replied, sounding subdued.

'Was there anything else?' Steve asked as she lapsed into silence.

'I really am very grateful for the way you looked after Lucy the night she was ill,' Ronnie said in a rush. 'Xan is, too, and he asked me to add his apologies and gratitude. He would have been with me today but his bike's playing up, so I walked. I don't think I've left anything out, have I?'

'For someone who hasn't had much practice at this sort of thing, I have to admit you grovel rather well.' Steve half-smiled at her.

Ronnie looked less confident than usual as she added, 'I don't know what I would have done if anything had happened to Lucy. She is the light of my life.'

'That I don't doubt,' Steve said in a softer voice.

'I've decided in future to be more hands-on. As soon as Xan can sort out accommodation for us, I plan to leave the commune.'

'You do?'

'I'm not deserting the cause or anything like that, but I realise it's time Lucy had a more stable background. She's growing up and she needs a proper home.'

'I'm pleased to hear it,' Steve said. 'She's an intelligent child.'

'I'm actually thinking of getting involved in local politics. I know it'll mean a lot of hard work and I'll probably hate not being on the front line, but — ' A rueful smile softened her lips. ' — it's time I settled down.' Ronnie shrugged her shoulders. 'So there you have it, except I forgot to add that the family had no idea what Jed was up to. Poor Babs was so embarrassed when Alison outed him.'

'Hm.' Steve looked thoughtful. 'I'm afraid Alison rather used us all.'

'What do you mean?' A frown wrinkled Ronnie's forehead.

'She realised early on that it was Jed who was the agent. He may have told her. I don't know what passed between them. Perhaps they discussed it during their time in America. Whatever, Alison knew it obviously wasn't me. She played everyone off against everyone else. I suppose she thought if she could stir things up against me then reveal the true identity of the culprit, well . . . ' Steve made a gesture with his hands. 'You don't need me to go into further detail. We all know what happened. She outwitted us all.'

'Do you think she did all this just to get back together with you?'

'I know it's a matter of habit with you, but there's no need to sound quite so surprised that a female should find my company desirable,' Steve reproached Ronnie.

'I'm only annoyed I fell for her story in the first place.'

'You always had me cast as the villain of the piece, and what she told you fitted in nicely with your theories.'

'I've learned my lesson,' Ronnie admitted. 'From now on the name of the game will be reasoned negotiation.'

The expression on Steve's face

betrayed his reservations but he said nothing.

'I have to hand it to Alison.' There was reluctant admiration in Ronnie's voice. 'She stage-managed the situation like a pro.'

'I hate to agree with you, but yes she did.'

'She certainly took the wind out of my mother's sails.'

'And some,' Steve acknowledged.

'I'm outraged that she used me and my companions in the way she did. I've had to apologise to just about everybody on the planet.'

'They say no experience is wasted.'

Ronnie twisted her straw hat in a gesture of uncertainty.

'Was there anything else?' Steve asked. 'Only, I am expecting a conference call with South America shortly.'

'You do know what happened had nothing to do with Hannah, don't you?' Ronnie asked in a rush, as if she were scared she was going to lose her nerve.

A shutter came down over Steve's

face. 'I never suspected for a moment that she was in any way involved,' he replied. 'Now, I really must prepare for my conference call.'

'Have you got a new housekeeper?' There was a desperate note in Ronnie's voice now.

'I am using an agency until things get sorted out.'

'What about Hannah?'

'You can reassure her that she is free to seek employment elsewhere.'

'What about the terms of her contract?'

'I won't be invoking them. I deduced after her swift disappearance from the scene that she no longer wished to work here. I really do need someone I can rely on, and neither Hannah nor your mother have proved to be reliable.'

Ronnie chewed her lip thoughtfully. 'Do you want to know where Hannah is?' she asked.

'I do not.'

'I could find out for you if you like.'

'I'm quite capable of discovering her

whereabouts for myself, but at the moment I don't choose to.' Steve stood up, indicating the visit was at an end. 'So, if you've said all you came here to say, we'd both best get on. Thank you for your visit. I appreciate the gesture.'

'You've heard Farmer Tony's made the field available to us again?' Ronnie seemed reluctant to move despite Steve's pressing body language. 'It won't take long to set things up again. Numbers are down, as some people have made other arrangements, but it will always be a refuge for those who want to come and join us.'

'Well, best of luck.' Steve opened the conservatory door.

'Are you coming to the party?' Ronnie asked.

'What party?'

'Midsummer's eve. It's in a week's time. Tony and Carol are holding a party to celebrate our return. They thought midsummer was a nice time because we can light a bonfire to keep warm, then stay up to watch the sunrise on midsummer's day. It's always a magical moment. There'll be a vegetarian barbecue, and music and dancing, and lots of love and laughter. You absolutely have to come.'

'My days of dancing until dawn are long over,' Steve admitted.

'Don't be such a stuffed shirt.' Ronnie was getting back into her stride as she added, 'It's a sad day when you fail to notice the beauty and love around you. It will be a good chance to re-bond with Deneham. The community needs a bit of togetherness after all we've been through. Everyone's confidence has been shattered.'

'It doesn't make much difference whether you think I'm being a stuffed shirt or not.' Ronnie flinched as Steve repeated her words. 'I'm scheduled for another visit to South America so I doubt I'll even be in the country the night of the party.'

'Promise me you'll come if you are?' Ronnie pleaded. 'I know Lucy would love to see you again. She's always talking about you.'

'I'll think about it.'

'You needn't worry that you'll bump into Hannah,' Ronnie added. 'She doesn't do sunrises either.'

'And that makes her a stuffed shirt too, does it?' Steve enquired with a sardonic raise of his eyebrow.

'My sister has always liked her beauty sleep.' There was a wistful note in Ronnie's voice as she added, 'And she is beautiful, only some people don't recognise the fact.'

A small muscle twitched under Steve's right eye.

'Don't let me keep you from your South American call.' Ronnie tugged at her tassels again. 'I'll see myself out.'

Standing on Steve's doorstep, a frown creased Ronnie's forehead. Her assurances that Steve wouldn't bump into Hannah at the party weren't entirely accurate, as she didn't know where her sister was. Babs told her before she left for America that she had met up with Hannah but had been sworn to secrecy as to her whereabouts. She also told Ronnie she had asked Hannah to contact her, but to date Ronnie had heard nothing.

They had never fallen out so seriously before. Like all sisters they had minor differences of opinion and occasions when they didn't speak to each other for a little while, but things always blew over when they both came to their senses. But this falling out was different.

Ronnie knew she was at fault. She should have realised the true nature of Alison's motives and not allowed herself to be influenced by her arguments against Steve. Learning that all plans to excavate in the area had been scrapped wasn't the success Ronnie hoped it would be. The news had come as a bitter victory. She'd lost her sister's trust, upset her mother and betrayed Steve, who had been a true friend at a time of family crisis. She had never felt more wretched in her life. The only person who still loved her unconditionally was Lucy, and even she had looked at her mother reproach-fully when yet another day had passed without a visit from her beloved aunty Hannah.

If any members of the commune knew where her sister was, they weren't saying. Ronnie's enquiries were met with a wall of silence. She could only hope that given time, Hannah would eventually come round.

Ronnie looked up at the sky. It promised to be another beautiful day, but she had never felt less like enjoying the sunshine. With a heavy heart she walked down Steve's drive. If she had turned round she would have noticed the face at the window following her progress. Steve's expression mirrored Ronnie's and he too looked as though he were in no mood to enjoy another blissful summer's day.

The iron gate creaked as Ronnie dragged it open. It still bore the battle-scars caused by the commune's protest. She ran her fingers over the damaged paintwork. It felt rough under her skin. In the distance she heard a dog barking. It sounded like Harlequin. Patti Morris was another resident Ronnie had fallen out with over her protests.

Ramming her straw hat back on her head, she decided the only way she could get back into everyone's good books was to start behaving responsibly, and that meant getting to grips with her new plans to be a councillor — a prospect she wasn't entirely looking forward to, but she was prepared to buckle down and work hard. Maybe then Hannah would realise just how much Ronnie wanted to make amends for all she had done.

As for Steve Talbot, Ronnie's lips tightened. He was a tough nut to crack, but there had to be a way she could get him to realise that he and Hannah were so right for each other. She knew it was none of her business and she foresaw fireworks, but it would be good practice for her negotiating skills to get them back together.

The beginning of an idea began to take seed in her mind and, feeling more confident, Ronnie strode down the lane back in the direction of the commune.

18

The sound of music drifted across the night air. Patricia Morris glanced at Hannah with an inquisitive smile. The light was fading from the day but it was too warm an evening to sit inside. Gnats buzzed around the sweet-scented honeysuckle, their dark silhouettes black smudges in the twilight.

'Aren't you going to the party?' Patricia broke the silence between them.

Hannah shook her head. 'I don't think so,' she replied in a disinterested voice.

'Farmer Tony said everyone was welcome.' Patricia was referring to the flyer that had been posted through their door earlier in the week announcing the midsummer festival.

'Are you going?' Hannah asked.

'There might be fireworks later and

256

they unsettle Harlequin. I think it's best I stay here and keep an eye on him, but there's no stopping you if you'd like to go. Don't feel you have to stay here to keep me company.' Patricia paused. 'And far be it from me to interfere, but don't you think it's time you made things up with Ronnie?'

'She's the one who should be apologising to me for all the trouble she caused.' Hannah knew she sounded petulant, but Ronnie's treachery still hurt.

'She doesn't know where you are,' Patricia pointed out.

'She could easily find out.'

'Your mother was most distressed the last time she rang.' Patricia tried another tack. 'I had to tell her the two of you were still not speaking to each other.' Patricia cast Hannah a sly look. 'It's little Lucy I feel sorry for. She must miss you dreadfully.'

'I miss her too,' Hannah admitted, wriggling uncomfortably in her wooden garden seat.

'Then for the sake of the little girl? I know family can be infuriating at times, but one of you has to swallow their pride.'

Hannah looked down to the end of the garden. Pinpricks of fairy lights twinkled in the trees and she could hear the crackling of the bonfire. Through gaps in the trees she could see red and yellow flames flickering around its base. Gentle white smoke billowed out in lazy curls as twigs snapped.

Hannah had watched volunteers working on their masterpiece over the past week. Overhanging branches had been cut down then lugged across the field amid much laughter. Children had run round picking up dead leaves, dry bits of wood and any other kindling they could find. Hannah had longed to join in but stubbornness prevented her. These were the people who had changed her life by chaining themselves to Steve's gate. These were the people who had caused her many a sleepless night with their false accusations. These were the people who had lost her a job she loved.

A part of Hannah hoped that Steve would have contacted her, if only to clear the air between them, but she had heard nothing from him either. She was now beginning to realise that that part of her life was over, but the thought of never seeing Steve again clogged her throat. His future was planned out with Alison. The two of them would probably lead a fabulously international life doing exciting things together.

Alison had outmanoeuvred Hannah on every score. She had been silly to entertain the idea that Steve could feel for her the same way she felt for him. Nothing had passed between them that could be remotely construed as romantic, and she had no right to indulge in silly daydreams.

Hannah wished she had never been talked into accepting the post of housekeeper at Highworth House, but the clincher had been when Steve had been kind enough to offer Lucy a home too, in spite of Ronnie's spirited stance against him. It took a special man to do that and Hannah had let any chance of a relationship slip through her fingers.

Deserting the house hadn't been her finest hour and she was beginning to realise that running away had been an error of judgement and totally unprofessional behaviour. If only she had been more experienced in matters of the heart, maybe she would have stayed on and tried to convince Steve that what had happened outside the house was nothing to do with her and possibly they had a future together, but from the moment Alison had grabbed the microphone on the day of the protest Hannah had known she would be fighting a lost cause.

The smell of scorched bracken was now mixed with the earthy aroma of roasting jacket potatoes. Hannah closed her eyes, imagining the scene in the field. Ronnie loved to party and soon the singing would start. In the past Hannah had enjoyed many such an evening, sitting round a campfire or dancing under the stars. She wasn't a very good dancer but no one had ever minded. Her singing voice wasn't up to much either, but everyone had joined in not caring who hit the wrong notes when it came to the tricky bits.

Her heart ached. How could she explain to Patricia that the real reason she couldn't go to the party was not because of Ronnie, but the prospect of bumping into Steve? She couldn't face him.

'They've got a lovely evening for their party.' Patricia was clearly not in the mood to give up. 'And it looks like Farmer Tony and Carol haven't done things by halves. They've erected a marquee and there's beer on tap for the men, ginger wine and soft drinks for the children.'

All day volunteers had been adding to the bonfire and it now resembled a miniature tower. It would require constant stoking if they were to keep it alight until dawn. Hannah's fingers itched to join them. Her mouth watered at the thought of the potatoes cooking in the ashes of the bonfire. She could imagine slicing one open and watching the steam rise, as she mashed in warm butter and melted cheese.

'I really ought to go over my CV.' Hannah shook off any longings she might have for a baked potato supper. 'I've got that interview with the call centre on Monday.'

Patricia made a dismissive noise at the back of her throat.

'It's the only interview I've been offered so far,' Hannah pointed out. 'I can't afford to turn it down.'

'That's as may be, but it's Saturday night. At your age I was out painting the town red.'

In the background someone began to strum a guitar. Hannah hesitated by the open windows.

'If you won't go,' Patricia sighed, 'then I can't force you, but I think you're making a big mistake.'

'I can stay and look after Harlequin

for you if you want to put in an appearance,' Hannah offered. 'I'm sure they'd let you come home before sunrise,' she added with a smile, 'if you get tired.'

'No thank you, but if you must be a party pooper then it's up to you. I shall sit here and listen to the music for a bit. It's far too nice an evening to be cooped up indoors hunched over a computer screen.'

'We could have some wine later,' Hannah coaxed. 'Isn't there a bottle in the fridge?'

'If you can drag yourself away from your CV.' Patricia turned her back on Hannah. With a sigh Hannah went indoors and booted up her laptop. Her life was at a crossroads and she had some serious thinking to do. In the past she had been able to turn to Ronnie or her mother for help, but both those avenues were now closed. She couldn't stay at the Willows with Patricia for much longer. It wasn't fair on her and she needed to get on with her life. Babs wanted Hannah to pay a visit to Texas at Hal's expense, but Hannah needed to sort things out at home first.

More music drifted through the open window and Hannah found it difficult to concentrate on her employment history. There wasn't much extra to add and it failed to hold her concentration. She couldn't help thinking about the party in the field. There was something magical about midsummer, the height of the year. Last midsummer she and Ronnie had sat up, she remembered to watch the dawn. Xan and his bikers had been there, together with Etaine, Tony and Carol and most of the commune. This year she was sitting alone in her room staring at a flicking computer screen.

A sudden explosion and a shower of pink stars made her jump. She looked through the open window and watched a rocket explode into the night sky. She hadn't expected the firework show to start so early. A chorus of oohs and aahs followed as a cascade of green, pink, silver and gold balls descended to the ground.

Down on the terrace she could hear Harlequin barking frantically. She frowned. Patricia had said she would keep an eye on him, but it sounded as though he was disturbed by the noise.

'Patricia?' she called out. 'Need any help?' There was no reply. Harlequin stopped mid-bark and everything went silent. Instincts aroused, Hannah went downstairs.

'Where is everybody?' she called out, making her way onto the terrace.

Harlequin's squashy toy had been abandoned under the sun lounger. Hannah bent down to pick it up.

'Hello.' Patricia appeared from the kitchen. 'I went in search of that bottle of wine,' she said. 'I thought I'd treat myself to a glass. Would you like one?'

'Where's Harlequin?' Hannah demanded.

Patricia looked round. 'He was here a moment ago.'

'I know. I heard him barking.'

'Harlequin?' Patricia put down her bottle and began to call out his name.

'Have you got a torch?' Hannah demanded.

'Somewhere, but I think the battery's flat. I've been meaning to replace it for ages but what with recent events it went completely out of my head. He's probably hiding under a bush. I thought they'd be setting off the fireworks later, otherwise I wouldn't have left him. I'll turn up the spotlight.' There was no sign of the dog in the garden, or the house. Patricia now began to look seriously worried.

'The fireworks must have upset him.'

'Where do you think he could have gone?' Hannah asked.

'He could be in the back field.'

'With the commune?'

'He couldn't get out the front gate. The side door is locked too, and he can't get through, but he could get over the back.'

'Wouldn't the fireworks have scared him off?'

'Would you go and take a look for me, Hannah?' Patricia pleaded. 'I know you said you didn't want to go to the party, but could you ask around if anyone's seen him? Fireworks do upset him so.'

'What are you going to do?'

'I'll ring round and ask if any of the neighbours have seen him. He may have got into one of their gardens. Please, Hannah. You can go across the field. There's a connecting gate.'

With her heart thumping painfully in her chest, Hannah picked her way through the darkness calling out Harlequin's name as she headed towards the party.

The noise grew louder as she approached the field and she could feel the rising heat from the bonfire. The firework display had now finished and people had started dancing and singing again. She looked round helplessly. Where would Harlequin go? One or two of the revellers recognised her and waved in Hannah's direction.

'Have you seen a dog?' she asked them.

'Sorry, no,' they apologised.

'Mrs Morris's crossbreed spaniel? Answers to the name of Harlequin.'

'If we see him we'll let you know,' they promised. 'Good to see you, Han,' another voice called out. 'The party hasn't been the same without you. Ronnie's round the bonfire with Xan. Go and say hello.'

Taking a deep breath, Hannah headed in the direction of the bonfire. A group of people was sitting in a circle singing songs. It wasn't difficult to make out Xan's bushy beard. Ronnie was sitting by his side leaning her arm on his knee, listening to the ballad being strummed on a guitar. Hannah took another step forward.

'So you've finally decided to show your face?'

Hannah swung round. Steve was standing behind her. In the background she could hear the bonfire collapsing as the flames took hold.

19

Hannah stumbled on an exposed tree root and Steve put a hand out to steady her. The next moment she was in his arms, the palms of her hands crushed against his chest. His checked shirt felt rough under her fingertips and the smell of wood smoke made Hannah's head swim.

'You haven't answered my question.' His hands were clamped around her upper arms in a vice-like grip, making it impossible for her to move.

'What are you doing here? Ronnie said you weren't coming.'

'I'm . . . ' Her voice cracked. 'I'm looking for Harlequin.'

'Who's Harlequin?'

'Mrs Morris's dog. He was spooked by the fireworks and ran away. You haven't seen him?'

'No I haven't seen him,' he replied

with a hollow laugh. 'For one insane moment I actually thought you might have come to the party to apologise for walking out on me. I should have known better.'

'I didn't know you'd be here,' Hannah protested. 'I didn't even know if you were in the country.'

Steve pushed her away and held her at arm's length, his eyes devouring every detail of her appearance. 'I know bonfire flames can do strange things to people's faces, but there are dark circles under your eyes and you've lost weight.'

'Is it surprising?' Hannah retaliated.

'Not really, no; with all that's been happening I suppose it isn't.' Steve took a deep breath, then asked, 'So, if you haven't run off with a new boyfriend, when are you coming back to High-worth House?'

'I'm not.'

'You can't let me down again.'

'I can, and you needn't quote the conditions of that wretched contract at me. Sue me if you like. I haven't any

270

money so you'd be the loser.'

'Has Ronnie been getting at you?' The expression on Steve's face also looked distorted in the light of the bonfire.

'I haven't spoken to my sister since before the demonstration.'

'I'd heard the two of you had fallen out.'

'Who told you that?'

'She did actually.'

'When?'

'Ronnie came to the house.'

'She did?' Hannah had difficulty keeping the surprise out of her voice.

'To thank me, to apologise, and I suspect to try to get us together again.'

'I don't believe you.' Hannah's heartbeat thumped against her chest.

'That's your privilege of course, but I am telling the truth.'

Hannah flushed. She hadn't meant to sound rude, but she was finding it difficult to think properly. Her head was in a whirl.

'If you have been speaking to Ronnie,

you'll know we fell out because of the demonstration.'

'She did mention it.'

'Did she also tell you it was nothing to do with me?' Hannah challenged Steve.

'She did, and I'd like to believe both of you, but if that's the case why did you walk out without a word?'

'You saw Alison's interview. Everything she said was true.'

'Correct me if I'm wrong, but I don't recall her saying you were part of the rabble outside the gate.'

'Don't call Ronnie's friends a rabble.'

'How would you describe them?'

'They're free-thinking individuals.'

'You now support their cause?'

'No, I mean I support the freedom of the individual.'

'You are beginning to sound like Ronnie.'

'Stop confusing me.' Hannah ran a hand over her forehead. With Steve staring at her so intently she couldn't think straight.

'Incidentally, where were you while Ronnie was busy gluing herself to anything that moved?'

'If you must know,' Hannah mumbled, 'I was behind the curtains.'

Steve threw back his head and laughed.

'What's so funny?' Hannah demanded.

'You are. One minute you're doing the freedom march bit, the next you're admitting you were scared and hiding behind the curtains.'

'I was not hiding, neither was I scared.' Hannah was outraged that Steve could think such a thing.

'That's not how I'm seeing it.'

'The police told me to lie low and that's exactly what I did. I was protecting your property in case things got overheated.'

'I'm sorry you had to go through all that,' Steve said. There was no trace of banter in his voice now. 'Why didn't you tell me what was in the wind?'

'Because I didn't want you haring back from Peru, or wherever it was you were. I hoped things would blow over, and if it hadn't been for Alison they might have done.' Hannah stopped speaking. Had she gone too far criticising Alison? 'I didn't mean — ' she began.

'Sometimes I have difficulty believing you and Ronnie are sisters,' Steve mused.

'I have difficulty believing it too,' Hannah admitted. 'She's the one with all the chutzpah, while I'm the quiet one, but I somehow always seem to get dragged along in her wake. It was the same with my mother.'

'That's family for you. And it doesn't matter — I love you the way you are.'

A stray firework exploded and for a second all Hannah could see was stars in her eyes. 'What was that you said?' She shook her head.

'I said I love you the way you are.'

'No.' Hannah took a firm step backwards.

'I know a muddy field and a smelly bonfire aren't the ideal venues for this sort of thing, but I'm scared if I don't say something now you'll run out on me again.'

'Alison, what about Alison?'

'Alison's history,' Steve said, 'and I'd be grateful if you didn't mention her name.'

'Mrs Morris said you were on the front page of the local newspaper announcing your engagement.'

'Mrs Morris got it wrong.' Steve's lips were compressed into a tight line.

'You're not an item?'

'We never were.'

'Was there really a clause in my mother's contract requiring me to find a new housekeeper if she didn't fulfil the terms and conditions of her employment?' Hannah asked as she began to realise it might be possible that Steve returned her feelings.

'I haven't read all the small print in detail, but let's not go into all that now. We've better things to talk about, wouldn't you say?'

'Then I can take that as a no?'

Hannah couldn't resist teasing.

'If you must,' Steve replied. 'I have to admit it was the only way I could stop you from joining that wretched commune.'

'What would you have done if my mother hadn't gone off and got herself married?'

'I expect I'd have thought of something equally brilliant. Now where were we?'

A shadowy movement behind Steve's shoulder caught Hannah's attention. 'I thought it was you,' a voice interrupted them.

Hannah peered into the darkness. 'Ronnie?'

Her sister took careful steps towards her. 'Sorry to interrupt and all that. Stop wriggling,' she reprimanded the animal she was cradling.

'You've found Harlequin.' Hannah held out her arms and the excited dog delivered a warm lick on her cheek as she and Ronnie tried to hug each other.

'It's so good to see you, Han. I'm

going to have to put Harlequin down. He's being a pest.'

'Patricia was so worried he'd run away. She sent me over here to look for him. I have to take him back.'

'No you don't,' Steve butted into the reunion. 'Ronnie can do that, as she found him. We've some unfinished business to discuss.'

'Where did you find him?' Hannah asked.

A look of pure guilt spread over Ronnie's face.

'Ronnie?' Hannah demanded. 'You didn't kidnap him?'

'I did, sort of,' she admitted. 'It's a long story but I heard Patti telling you about the fireworks and how they upset Harlequin.'

'You must have good hearing,' Steve said. 'The field's not that close.'

'I'd gone the back way round to the Willows. I suspected that was where Han was holing out and I had to see her.'

'Go on,' Hannah urged.

'I hid in the garden for a bit while I decided what to do.' She grimaced. 'I'm not coming out of this very well, am I?'

'I don't know about Hannah, but I'm finding it very entertaining.' Steve crossed his arms. 'Do continue.'

'I wanted to make things up with you, Han, but after what you said to Patti about me I knew it wasn't going to be easy.' Ronnie took a deep breath. 'Anyway, when you went inside — ' Ronnie's look of misery deepened. ' — Patti and I hatched a plot.'

'You mean she was in on it?' Hannah could hardly believe what Ronnie was telling her.

'I'll admit she took a bit of persuading, and she got the fright of her life when I emerged from the bushes, but when I explained Harlequin wouldn't be hurt she was up for it. I hope you didn't think I stole the dog to get back at Patti?'

'I don't know what to think anymore,' Hannah replied in a faint voice.

'Look, I'll make myself scarce,'

Ronnie suggested. 'I'm sure you and Steve have lots to talk about. I'll take Harlequin home before Patti starts to get worried, then why don't you join us for the sunrise ceremony? Please, Han?' she pleaded.

'Do as she says,' Steve put in. 'I'm sure Ronnie is dying to tell you all about her plans to go into local government.'

'What?'

A familiar impish smile crossed Ronnie's face. 'You'd better believe it.' She grinned.

'Harlequin?' a faint voice echoed through the darkness. 'Where are you?'

'Sounds like Patti.' Ronnie brushed Hannah's cheek with her lips. 'Don't let me down. We're having a kissing ceremony at daybreak. I know it sounds a bit yucky, but after all the upset over the recent weeks, Deneham needs to re-bond. Lucy's going to be there and you wouldn't want to disappoint your niece, would you? Coming,' she trilled as she caught sight of Patricia Morris.

'By the way, sunrise is a time for lovers too.'

'You just invented that,' Hannah called after Ronnie.

'Prove it,' she laughed.

'What do you make of all that?' Hannah turned back to Steve.

'It's not often I find myself in agreement with your sister.' He took her gently in his arms. 'But why don't we start getting in some practice for this kissing ceremony?'

'You mean you're staying on for it?'

'I haven't anything better to do, have you?'

The last of the fireworks exploded into the night sky as Steve took Hannah in his arms.

'Did you mean what you said about being in love with me?' Hannah asked him.

'Don't you believe me?'

'You haven't asked me if I feel the same way about you.'

'Do you?' Steve asked.

'Yes.' Hannah's answer was little

more than a whisper. 'But are you sure you know what you're letting yourself in for, getting involved with my family?'

'A lifetime of fireworks, I should imagine,' Steve replied with a wry smile before his lips descended on Hannah's.

THE END

We do hope that you have enjoyed
reading this large print book.

Did you know that all of our titles
are available for purchase?

We publish a wide range of high
quality large print books including:
Romances, Mysteries, Classics
General Fi
Non Fiction a

Special interest ti
large pri
The Little Oxfo
Music Book,
Hymn Book, S

Also available fro
Oxford Univ
Young Reader
(large prin
Young Reader
(large prin

For further inform
brochure, please contact us at:
Ulverscroft Large Print Books Ltd.,
The Green, Bradgate Road, Anstey,
Leicester, LE7 7FU, England.
Tel: (00 44) 0116 236 4325
Fax: (00 44) 0116 234 0205